THE

DISAPPEARED

ADAM

BRAVER

A

NOVEL

Outpost19 | San Francisco
outpost19.com

Braver, Adam
        The Disappeared / Adam Braver
        ISBN: 9781944853341 (pbk)

Library of Congress Control Number: 2017910726

OUTPOST19

ORIGINAL
PROVOCATIVE
READING

Also by
Adam Braver

Misfit
November 22, 1963
Crows Over The Wheatfield
Divine Sarah
Mr. Lincoln's Wars

Betty Braver
1944 – 2015

Philip Schild
1919 – 2015

THE DISAPPEARED

ADAM BRAVER

A

NOVEL

BOOK ONE

EDGAR
AND
LUCY

LUCY
FALL 2015

THE MORNING OF THE SHOOTING is the last day she'll go out for a while. Already Lucy had been growing nervous about being out in public. Following a season of international terror attacks, her daily routine had been thus: get in the car, drive to work, eat lunch inside the building, get in the car and come back home. There was no more gathering in large public spaces. No more train to work. The unseen risks outsized the convenience. She'd even conceded all grocery shopping to Henry, refusing to be a target in the Raley's parking lot or inside the crowded market. Think about it: at the time, who would have thought twice about sitting in a Parisian café on that warm November night? Or who would have had any apprehension about just waiting for the usual commuter train in the usual station at the usual time in London or Madrid? The cable news shows said we now lived in an era of vigilance. Lucy saw it more as an era of cautious retreat. And cautious retreat wasn't always so easy. Just when she'd have her routine managed, something else would pop up, and she'd be forced to adjust on the fly, fighting her instinct just to let it go. It was a little like having to change your diet following a sudden health scare—despite knowing what must be done, it still takes total vigilance and will to alter all your habits and desires. Her most recent challenge had been

1

this past weekend's trip to Southern California. Henry had planned it months ago. He'd had a conference there, and he figured it made a nice excuse for them to be at the beach before he started on Monday. In spite of her cautious retreat, she'd been stuck having to go. There were few reasonable excuses Lucy could conjure up that didn't convey hysteria. So in the days leading up to the flight, she summoned all her strength. Took deep breaths. Visualized normal days. Avoided the TV news. And she told herself it was only for a weekend. Together they navigated the airport and rented a car, and then took an overnight stay at Newport Beach. Once in motion, the getaway turned out fine. Enough so, that over Saturday night dinner she declared her anxiety as stupid and misguided. She'd told Henry she realized that she'd been held hostage by anticipation. The next evening, she emailed Henry to report that she'd gotten home safely. And maybe she got carried away, distracted from vigilance by the ease and seduction of believing herself safe on the Pacific beach, but in her email she suggested coming back down the following Friday when Henry's obligations ended. They'd have another weekend there, and together they could come back on Sunday. *Statistically*, she added, *Sundays are the safest days of the week.*

But on the morning of the shooting, Lucy is alone, and when she's alone she moves a little more languidly. Takes her time, even when she knows she shouldn't. It's a little cloudy out, making the morning a bit darker than normal. Her telephone rings, and it is a private number, one that she assumes is Dr. Shore, calling to confirm the blood test taken last Thursday.

Although she is at the point where she should be starting the car, Lucy still is in her bathrobe, staring at the ringing phone, debating whether or not she has time to answer it. Her boss, Edith Franks, a career State employee who seems to evade retirement no matter who is the Secretary of State in the current cycle, manages and judges based on adherence to the clock, with little interest in the work itself. It's a stupid thing to play in to, Lucy knows. But one that still promotes anxiety about being late, as the consequence is a day-long series of undercutting comments about time management and responsibility. But because she and Henry are awaiting the results of the pregnancy test, pins and needles all weekend long, she picks up the phone, already nervous that the news only will make her later, as she'll have to call Henry, surely at the conference by now for the early breakfast buffet.

But on the morning of the shooting, it is not Dr. Shore on the other end. It is Sarina. Sarina, who sits two offices down, and sometimes works the research desk with her. Sarina, who also has figured out how to have her phone read *Private Caller* because she says there are too many psychos out there. Sometimes Lucy thinks Sarina secretly worries no one would pick up her calls otherwise. Although she is well-meaning and desperately committed to friendship, Sarina can have an enthusiasm that often finds her mistaken for being an alarmist. More than likely she's just excited to tell you something that's popped into her head.

Immediately upon hearing Sarina's voice, Lucy says, "Sarina, can it wait for a half hour? I'm trying to get out the door." Usually Mondays are reserved for Sarina to deconstruct a bad date from the weekend, break down her latest goofy adventure, or to prosecute some injustice that found its way to her. But it is rare for it to come before work. Typically, it's a whisper in the cubicle. Over coffee in the cafeteria. By the elevator in the first floor foyer, where they wait instead of taking the stairs up to the fourth.

Lucy can hear the echo chamber of the speaker phone in the car. It makes Sarina sound as though she is shouting into the entrance of a cave. The radio murmurs and crackles in the background. And a siren wails by, to which Sarina suddenly yells, "Jesus, buddy. You pull over when you hear an ambulance."

Stepping over the threshold of her closet door, a sneaker propped to hold it open, still not sure what she'll wear today, Lucy tells Sarina she'll find her first thing when she gets to work. Her eyes scan the built-in shelves, clothes neatly folded and slightly shoved in. She says, "I promise, first thing. I just need to get out the door."

"Well, then turn on the TV. Turn it on while you finish getting ready. It's just too awful. Really scary. And I know you were just there yesterday. And I know Henry is on business down there. And I know . . . That's why I'm calling. To check."

"What are you . . .?"

"You'll let me know everything is okay when you get to work. You'll let me know. Promise?"

Lucy hangs up the phone, a little bewildered, a little bit thrown by Sarina's urgency, and by her having brought Henry's business trip into it. But then she has to keep in mind what a mixer Sarina is, and how her life reduced down to a mathematical formula would be *Day* − *Drama* = *Dull*. Nevertheless, Sarina's call has riled her. Trying to rush, she plucks her brown tights and matching dress out of the closet. And even though she knows it will make her late, Lucy lays the garments across her side of the bed, and then grabs the remote off the nightstand.

The morning of the shooting, the television turns into the antagonist. It will be impossible to turn off. It will become the realization of those predictions about how it would suck people in, hypnotizing them, turning them catatonic, and possessing them through the power of images and flickering rays and the blue lights that disrupt the body's natural circadian rhythms by gumming up the melatonin. And on the TV she will see the familiar architecture of the town where Henry is visiting for work. From the perspective of a helicopter she will see a building that bears no relation to the type of work Henry does, but then the newscaster will say that unconfirmed sources say that many public groups and organizations use the building for trainings and conferences, and then give examples of the types that have been there in the past. Who was there today only would be speculation. All she knows is that Henry was conducting a training *at* a conference, and suddenly she is two-for-two—three-for-three, if you include the town—and she thinks maybe it can go away if she just turns off the TV, and so she pushes the red button on the remote once, but nothing happens, and so she does it again, double-pumping, and finally the TV clicks off, fading into black. Yet just when the remaining light narrows to a little circle in the middle of the screen, she hears a subtle burst of crackling electronics, and the screen opens up again with the sound of the chop-chop-chopping of the helicopter blades and the view of the building that sometimes houses trainings and conferences.

She reaches for the telephone, the receiver still warm from Sarina's call. Too flustered to remember Henry's number, Lucy flips through the contacts wildly and randomly, as though trying to find a stranger's name in a strange city's phone book.

The morning of the shooting, Henry's phone will ring endlessly before going to voicemail. And Lucy will leave a message, adopting a tone that is somewhere between concern and terse; and when after four-and-a-half minutes he doesn't return the call, she again will leave the same basic message. And again when there is no response, she hits redial again, again, again, again, again, and again, not leaving any more messages because there is no time for such a thing.

Lucy has forgotten about going to work. Forgotten about Edith Franks and her allegiance to the schedule. She even has forgotten to get changed. Sitting right atop her dress, one hand on the phone and the other on the remote, she is like one of those shadow outlines left after a blast, the morning's events exploded all around her.

All the news can say is that there has been a mass shooting, and there may be bombs planted, and everything is on lockdown. A terrorism expert joins the broadcast, a former higher-up in the FBI, and with a wide face that fills the screen he emphasizes that he has no information, but if this were the work of foreign terrorists, then we have every right to suspect that there may be simultaneous plots about to be hatched all across the country, because that is the nature of their thinking, to inflict the maximum harm and terror on the most people that they can. Didn't Paris show that? But still, he adds, and he says he must emphasize this, he only is speaking hypothetically, and the anchor interjects, "Just to be clear, there are no reports, ZERO sources that can tell us what kind of attack this might be."

The phone rings and she looks down to see *Private Caller*. Her first instinct is that it is Sarina, trying to figure out what is going on. In all fairness, Sarina probably does care, and by now she certainly has noticed that Lucy is not in the office; Sarina, who is no doubt badgered by Edith Franks, who would have stepped into her cubicle with an announcing cough and said, "I wonder how it is that some people just find it so difficult to be somewhere on time." And maybe Sarina will shrug and say she doesn't know any more than you, Edith; or maybe she will say something about the attack that is being reported and that Lucy's husband Henry is there, and because of that perhaps there are unknowns that Lucy needs to address or confirm, at which point Edith might say, "I'm sure she knows how to use the telephone or how to send me an email." But right now Lucy doesn't want to know. Doesn't care. It seems so unimportant, that part of life.

And it could be Dr. Shore, the other known *Private Caller*, but that is a call that Lucy also can't take. She is not sure she wants to know. At least right now. In part because she couldn't stand getting the news without immediately being able to share it with Henry, but also, because when she first turned on the TV, glued to the chaos and the ongoing confusion, she reached through her robe, rubbed her palm against her belly for some sense of contact, and at that moment instinctively knew that she wasn't pregnant. But that is not something she wants to discuss with Dr. Shore, whether she lost the baby or if there ever was a baby. It's better not to know. It's better not to know anything. In fact, Lucy thinks that maybe she should just go into work, take her lumps from Edith Franks, and research, copy, and prepare whatever requests have been made this morning to the Archives; keep a normal, normal day, because treating it as a normal, normal day will mean it's a normal, normal day, and at five o'clock, exactly when Edith Franks dismisses her team, Lucy can go home, and she will speak with Henry, just as it was meant to be.

But instead, on this morning of the shooting, she lowers herself back on to the bed, her eyes fixed on the television. It is still the view from the chopper, and at times the camera zooms in wobbly and grainy to the grounds surrounding the building where police and SWAT stand behind open car doors and large black command vehicles, poised and waiting, as though there is more to come. The voiceover says something about the bomb squad, and the shifting tenor of the scene, and how it still is unclear if it is an "active crime scene" or not. Lucy watches and watches and watches, and if it weren't for the flag flapping in the breeze at the entrance to the grounds, she would swear she was watching a still photo. She has stopped dialing and redialing Henry's phone, understanding that this may or may not be an "active crime scene," and that a ringing phone would do him no good if in fact he were there. Also it occurs to her that she should keep the line open. Their calls potentially could cross and cancel each other out.

The phone rings again. Three times over the next hour. Each time it is *Private Caller, Private Caller, Private Caller*. The first two she ignores. The third she answers, the ringing getting to her, and then immediately hangs up.

She rises, cinches tight her bathrobe, and then, still standing next to the bed, she leans over and first folds her stockings and then her dress at the indentation along the waist. Returning them to the closet, she tries to stack them neatly, even though one of the dress's arms dangles down.

This is only the morning of the shooting. And, as they keep repeating on the TV, there is so much we do not know. So much that still is unfolding.

Edgar
Summer 1993

EDGAR SEES HIM out the corner of his eye—reddish-brownish beard, a Confederate flag sticker on the windshield of his pick-up/living out in the suburbs/ screwed by the world kind of look. And it catches Edgar's attention because not only does that guy seem out of place among the protesters gathering at the east end of the State Capitol lawn, a semi-organized assemblage responding to a mass shooting in San Francisco that showed the current laws to be pure shit, but Edgar notices him facing upstream against the oncoming crowd—silent, with his palms upturned like he's the messiah. And shoved down the front of his pants he has a nightstick, and he pulls it out just as Edgar and Mildred are walking by.

The cretin has no particular target, more like a stick of dynamite whose fuse is lit and burning down, and fucker explodes right on Edgar, who hears the crack against his shoulder like it's something far off, and then another against his knee. Before the pain even registers, Edgar buckles over onto the ground, full weight on his hands, as his knees turn suddenly useless.

There's a pause, one that sounds almost musical. Extended. And then comes the whack against his skull. Flat. Like a sound without an echo.

His head turns really, really warm, and he's hearing

Mildred scream, and who can tell if it is *at* the guy or *for* Edgar, but he's going really woozy, and he really wants to close his eyes and get away from it all, just be gone, and he might have if there wasn't someone leaning over him, telling him, "Keep awake now. Stay with me. Tell me your name," and Mildred answers, "Edgar," and the voice, which brings with it a cologne that in waves jolts Edgar awake like it's a smelling salt, says, "We need to let him answer. Keep him talking and alert until the paramedics arrive."

Later, when Edgar is laid up and conscious in the hospital, during the first of her regular visits Mildred will note that Edgar kept calling her Erin, which is the name of his lost sister. Upon hearing that he'll swallow, and get a little sick to his stomach. Thinking about his missing sister can still undo him, in part because in the aftermath of the attack, Edgar has struggled to remember anything specific about her (although he has a vague, vague memory of having an important thought about her just as the attack took place). That loss of detail alone terrifies him more than the questions surrounding his recovery. Whatever he can't remember about his older sister, including whatever was on his mind when the nightstick clubbed him, could be one of any of the essential pieces that keeps his sister from ever being found after nearly a year.

You kept calling me Erin, You kept calling me Erin, You kept calling me Erin.

It is like another round of pummeling that plays over and over in his head, and much like the real beating, instead of hearing it, he'd really rather close his eyes, go away, and tune out all the voices that tell him to keep awake.

For the physical trauma, Dr. Merman has advised that if Edgar remains homebound and rests, regularly stretches and walks and ices and heats, coupled with eventual physical therapy, then they should see a gradual improvement over six months to a year. But the gaps and glitches to his memory are the worst part of the aftermath. Twenty-four is too young to stumble over remembering. And it seems to be random, with no set pattern. Sometimes it's something short term, other times events from his past. Names trouble him. Relationships stump him. Order of events. But what's most frustrated him to the point of anger is when he can almost always see the faint outline of each memory; he can reach out for one of them, but never quite grab it. Dr. Merman warned him this might happen, and if he didn't see marked improvement within four weeks then Edgar needed to be referred to a neurologist for further evaluation. So Edgar keeps it to himself. Tries to hide it from the purview of his mother, who, specifically because of question marks about self-determination in the days immediately following the head injury, was given temporary power of attorney over Edgar's health decisions and personal finances.

He doesn't want further testing; he doesn't want to know.

During week five, some past memories randomly begin to appear. A person. Place. A scene from a movie. The browned crust of a pastry from a specific bakery. Sometimes they are called up by a photo in the paper. Something he reads. A song he hears. And on the Thursday evening of that week, a story about New York City on the nightly news triggers a very specific memory of his sister. It's a revelation. Maybe what he'd been thinking when the club struck him. The missing piece. It is so vivid, and it's so crucial, that he wonders what damage to his sister might have been done in the intervening time that the memory had gone dormant.

He calls his mother. He says she needs to come over right away.

She says, "Just tell me now." Even though she lives less than ten miles away in her subdivision down by the American River, she's always refused to venture into midtown because she says there are too many bums, too many weirdos, and too many druggies.

He hears her sigh while lowering herself onto the kitchen stool, followed by the ting of the base of her wine glass against the counter. And without giving him time, she adds, "So what do you need to tell me so badly?"

He tells her that what he's remembered is this: he remembers having watched the news eight months earlier, February 26 to be exact, following the breaking coverage of the bombing in the parking garage of the World Trade Center. To his mother, from memory, he recites the names of all the terrorists involved ("Ramzi Yousef, Mahmud Abouhalima, Mohammed A. Salameh, Nidal A. Ayyad, Abdul Rahman Yasin, and Ahmed Mohammad Ajaj"). He quotes the report that said six people died and nearly a thousand more injured, and that it could have been much worse if the bombing had actually gone off as planned, a failed engineering feat that had been meant to send the south tower tumbling into the north tower.

His mother says, "You wanted me to drive all the way across town to tell me that?"

He says, "It's the next part. What we've been waiting for all year."

"Edgar, where is this going?"

He pulls the phone closer, lowering his voice. He explains that the revelatory part of the memory is that on the broadcast he clearly saw his limp sister being carried out of the Trade Tower by two responders, feet raised up high, head flopped back. Draped arms. Her fingers dragging along the dusty sidewalk.

"Stop this nonsense."

"Maybe she is in a coma."

"Stop this nonsense, stop this nonsense."

"Maybe it is amnesia. Maybe, maybe. Maybe Jane Doe in a New York hospital ward."

"I understand you mean well. And I know you still are recovering."

"I only know what I remember seeing. I can see it now. Plain as day. As though I'm watching it while we're talking."

"I think we need to call your doctor again . . . I'll arrange for your uncle to take you tomorrow."

He says, "She may be waiting for us. We don't have time. Erin probably is counting on us to rescue her."

"Stop this nonsense, stop this nonsense, stop this nonsense."

The following day, on the car ride home from the doctor's office, little is said between Edgar and his uncle, his late

14

father's younger brother. They are coming in north on 99, passing still undeveloped land with the holdouts of small farms. Short, stout, and impossibly gregarious with everyone he meets, his uncle is so different in demeanor and stature than Edgar's father ever had been. The lack of family resemblance is so markedly distinct that as kids Edgar's father took to calling his brother Pastor, which came from Pasteur, which came from milk, and at the bottom of that eponymous pyramid the "milkman's son"—a nickname that stuck and lived on as one small part of his father's legacy. Pastor had taken over the family company when Edgar's father died. Pastor loved being in the beer and beverage business his father had started, and he especially always relished the idea of what he called a "family industry," but he never had (nor has) any intention of ever running Duncan Distributors, as he prefers sales and being out and about with people, not sitting in a warehouse in an office buried within another office like Russian nesting dolls. Following his brother's death, even though Mrs. Duncan assumed the position of CEO of the company, Pastor assumed the leadership on an interim basis only on the assurance that Edgar would follow in his father's role once he graduated college. But that interim period extended when Edgar drifted into volunteer work at the social service agency after his recent graduation, further lengthened by the attack. Pastor's stake in his nephew's recovery has hardly been a secret.

The windows are rolled down and the air smells like hay, and it even looks a little yellow. Pastor says, "Did you hear what that doctor said?"

"Which part?"

His uncle pauses. It would seem as though he doesn't know if Edgar truly is confused or if he is being a smart ass. "*Confabulation*," he says, sounding out the word.

"Oh, that part."

"So then you must understand that the things you say about your sister, about this crazy notion about her and the Trade Towers . . . How it upsets your mother. We all know Erin always has had her own ideas. I like to believe she has no idea about all the pain she's caused. But now that you know how the head injury can alter memory, maybe you should just consider dialing it back a little. Keep your theories to yourself."

"I know what I remember."

"Jesus, Junior. There's even a medical name for it. Can't you see?"

Edgar rolls the window down farther. Like a dog, he pushes his face out and inhales the air, not quite fresh since they've merged onto 80. More exhaust than agriculture. Regardless, it makes him feel alive again. With purpose. And it's something he consciously tells himself to hold in. Because once he is back at his apartment, and his uncle is helping him up the stairs, and his knee feels like it will explode, and his balance will turn woozy and the thought of leaving again will sound like nothing short of agony, he will return back to this moment, with fresh air in his lungs, and his face warmed by the sun and preserved by the wind.

At the bottom of the exit on H Street, Edgar withdraws his head back into the cab, and lights up a smoke. He looks straight ahead. Finally, he responds to Pastor in what is his main defense, the same one he

16

so frustratingly tried to convince Dr. Merman of, who only heard the main defense as being symptomatic of *confabulation*. Speaking to Pastor as though Edgar wasn't in the room, Dr. Merman prescribed cognitive rehab in order reclassify Edgar's memories so he could gain control over distinguishing what was actually experienced, and what, post injury, the brain was telling him he experienced.

Staring out the window, and making a declaration as much for himself as for his uncle, Edgar reiterates, "I know what I remember." It seems so plainly obvious.

·

Edgar, the fallen angel. Once expected to be the embodiment of his father, who in front of Edgar and Erin, at ages eight-and-a-half and eleven, had dropped to his knees in the living room, grabbed at his chest, and then started pulling at his neck like he was trying to rip it open. His father then made a noise so mechanical that it seemed impossible to believe, even to this day, that it had come from a human being. Edgar, Sr. fell back, his open gaze fixed on the ceiling forever in a permanent state of frustration, something that would still emanate from this once powerful man when his eyes were closed, made up, and powdered in his casket the following weekend. Edgar, the fallen angel, who at the time Erin disappeared had his own kind of spiritual disappearance and questioned if he really wanted to be the incarnate of his father. Edgar, the lone crusader, who when visiting his mother's house has to see the photos of Erin, the closed door to what had been

17

her room, and is supposed to join the family chorus of having given up and *accepted*, even though he hasn't given up or *accepted*. Edgar, the fallen angel and the lone crusader, who has struggled so hard to remember Erin, and now sees what happened to her so clearly. A sense of vindication, but one stifled by doctors who tell him it is a false memory brought on by the beating to the head, and a mother who only can say, Stop this nonsense, stop this nonsense, stop this nonsense.

Somewhere in a box stacked upon other boxes in the utility room closet at his mother's house rests the last known photo of his sister, taken by Pastor a few years before Erin disappeared. In the snapshot, Edgar, his final year in high school, glares at the camera, arms crossed and backed into the corner, between the bookshelf and the deep mahogany hi-fi console that covers most of the white linen wall. About half the mingling faces are unidentifiable—Duncan Distributorship employees, along with their family members. His expression, in the center of the frame, is a new one he'd been working on: defiant boredom. One he had been perfecting. But look down to the bottom right corner of the photo, and on the couch sits his sister Erin. She looks phantasmagorical— her face nearly bleached white, while her dark black hair blends into the drawn curtains behind her. In a plain white short-sleeve linen shirt, a denim skirt and bare feet, Erin sits legs crossed, nestled against the corner arm of the brown couch, looking up momentarily, her hands suggesting that she's flipping through one of the magazines from the coffee table, impatiently turning pages as though they are hiding something. It's hard to read her expression. Certainly not one that betrays a plan. Or one that suggests any kind of portending farewell.

The photo will be taken in the middle of her junior year of college, and she will be at the house under protest, pressured by their mother to attend the annual Duncan Distributorship holiday party, a tradition started by their father to bring the most loyal employees into his own home as a gesture of welcome and trust, now hosted by their mother and their uncle, Pastor. Erin, who obsessively makes jewelry, pounding out steel earrings and stringing jade onto necklaces in the metal shop at school despite her mother thinking she should be studying to be a school teacher or something more befitting a girl of her upbringing, will have just lost a three-day battle with her mother, a sustained shouting match that involved Erin saying the family business was blood money that traded on people's addictions, a legalized form of drug dealing, one that only reinforced her disgust with the social structure, and something she had no interest in celebrating. And as the fight escalated, Erin would broaden her argument (sometimes sounding more like a plea) to say that like it or not there was no way she was following in her mother's footsteps— dashing around in cream-colored blazers and set hair, affecting bourgeois accents and appropriating socially correct conversation topics, changing furniture with the seasons in concert with interior designers who kiss cheeks and fake intimacies, and developing an instinct for when to excommunicate friends who make an indictable faux pas, change to a lesser spouse, or suffer emotionally in public. In other words, Erin yelled across the house, "In a million years I would never disgrace any woman by being that phony and that judgmental just to be accepted."

From his bedroom down the hall, Edgar would have heard his mother argue back, never raising her voice, but rather increasing the force of it in a near-invisible way that caused the museum of family photos along the hallway walls to vibrate and end up slightly off-kilter, each one eventually needing to be straightened out. The rebuttal was predictable. It noted the keys words such as "spoiled," "ungrateful," "nasty," and "brat." It said that Erin should get out all the screaming now. Before the holiday event.

On the day of the party, both had become the judge and the accused, often interchanging roles mid-argument. Each had every right to feel unfairly under attack, such was their brutality. And by evening, a détente had gone into effect. When Edgar came out from his room, they showered him with attention like he was absorbing stray and erratic electrical currents. He couldn't wait for the guests to arrive. It was obvious that there had been neither a victory nor a concession from either side. Instead, there was a shared resignation that a space was devolving.

Now look again at the photo: even when Erin is there, and even when she sits on the couch, magazine in hand, and even when she appears in the bottom corner of the photograph, already she is fading from view. That ghostliness, Edgar has always thought, was not a trick of the lens or the exposure. Instead, it was the capturing of an actual spirit just at the moment it was dissolving.

Someone said Erin's leaving was to escape further emotional damage done to her by her mother, started once she'd no longer been under her father's protection. Another theory was that it had nothing to do with rejection of the family values and promoting her own ideals, but instead that she'd fallen under the spell of an older man whom she trailed out to New York. But to this day what most has troubled Edgar is not that his mother and uncle accepted that Erin would up and leave for any one of those reasons, but how easily they would accept that she was never coming back.

•

"Here's a story for you: there once was a doctor and he thought he could tell you what you're thinking and remembering, tell you it's wrong and why, and then give it a name." He is saying this to Mildred, who has just walked into his apartment, as she has done every Friday evening since he returned home after the beating, bringing over Zelda's pizza. He is on the couch in his living room, a beige corduroy couch before a sculpted glass coffee table holding two small candlesticks and today's newspaper, still folded. To each side of the couch are matching chairs, and pushed against the wall is a medium size bookcase that houses not only current and well-reviewed titles, but ones whose spines curiously have various hues and shades that seem to accent the décor. Mildred kicks the door shut with her heel. She says, "It's what they do."

Since his uncle brought him home earlier in the afternoon, Edgar cannot stop dwelling on the insult of the doctor's appointment. He cannot stop thinking about the word. *Confabulation.* It is a bullshit word. It is a word that in and of itself is what it's trying to define. *Confabulation*. But what gets to him most is that because the congress of his mother, uncle, and doctor are so hooked on this, on proving *confabulation*, that the real issue of Erin being out there, perhaps even waiting for one of them, is not just being overlooked, but it is being dismissed.

Mildred puts the pizza on the dining room table, scooting it to the right of a lace runner that flows down the middle. She says she's sorry for getting there later than usual but that the wait was out of this world. "Is there something going on tonight?" she asks. "Some kind of sports event or something?"

He says, "Then why did you bother?"

"What?"

"If the wait was so long, why did you even bother?"

She lets out a long breath, trying not to betray how clearly irritated she is by his snappish remark. Turning her back on him, Mildred announces she'll be back in a moment. She's getting some plates and napkins from the kitchen. Although she tries to sound even and patient, her words come out clipped and jagged.

He calls out, "Mildred!" When they'd first met at the volunteer agency, he referred to her as Millie, and she'd corrected him to Mildred, which seemed too old and antiquated of a name for a twenty-three-year-old. Despite Edgar's protests for Millie, her protests for Mildred were louder, and thus he deferred to Mildred. Slowly, he got used to it, except for in her absence when he still finds himself visualizing a nineteenth-century woman cloaked in a prairie dress and pinafore, with a bonnet capping her head. "Mildred," he says again.

"They always pack napkins." It's an empty gesture, that he knows, but it's the best he can do by way of an apology. Right now, she is his only ally. The one person he can tell something to who isn't looking for a clue or an insight into his mental state.

He knows she feels responsible for what happened to him. He knows she believes she led him into a situation that he wouldn't have been in otherwise. It was her idea to go, and they'd barely known each other, but he'd gone on his own volition—partly because it was something to do, and partly because her countenance reminded him of his missing sister. Even though he's told her that he doesn't blame her for what happened at the Capitol, Mildred will not let go of the burden. Despite always trying to keep upbeat and positive, last week she confessed that the memory comes into her mind every single night as she is falling asleep, and though she felt stupid for saying it, given what Edgar was going through, it still was tearing her apart. And he told her he understood. He said it was okay, she should let it go. And because she is kind, he didn't bother to remind her that in spite of how it was "tearing her apart," still Mildred walks in. Mildred walks out. She knows fresh air. The smell of rain. The tedium of waiting at Zelda's for no apparent reason. The short steps up the stairs. Having to wash her hands after touching the handrail. In a typical hour Mildred has more experiences than he has had in total since returning home.

She brings him the pizza, taking a seat in the stuffed chair on the right. Edgar takes a bite, savoring the deep dish Chicago style of which he really likes the olive oil saturated cornbread crust. He chews slowly. His hearing is just off enough that the masticating sounds amplified, like boots marching over loose gravel. After he swallows, Edgar tells her thank you. "Thanks for waiting for the pizza."

She says, "Well, you know."

"It's just been a day."

"Now, you were saying about the doctor . . . When I came in."

He shakes his head. "Nothing," he says. "Just the usual. You know how doctors are. The medical industrial complex."

"Yeah, I guess, although I'm not really sure what that means."

Edgar edges over to the corner of the couch, closer to Mildred. He leans forward. "You are not going to believe it."

She pulls back slightly. Looking a bit unsure. "Okay," she says. "I think I'm ready."

"You know how my memory has been a little funky lately?"

"Edgar." She shakes her head. "That's not for me to say."

"Well it has, and we can both agree on that. But here is the thing, earlier this week it started clearing up a little. Things began coming back. In detail. Critical detail."

Mildred lets out a deep sigh. She tells him that's great. "Really good news."

"But that's not the half of it." He tells her about the Trade Center bombing and Erin, and for a moment he is beaming, reveling in sharing this major discovery with someone who can appreciate it, and someone who has no stake in judging or trying to disprove his case.

But then his face tightens, and along with that follows his whole body tensing, and his knee starts to throb so much that he can actually picture the bones exploding right through the skin. Like a reflex, he kicks his leg out to shoo away the pain. That small gesture causes an audible yelp.

Mildred stands, sliding her plate onto the coffee table. She asks if he's okay.

He waves her away. Directs her back to her chair. He says it's just the stress. He tells her he gets worked up thinking about his mother's reaction. "She's put everything about Erin behind her. Made a new talking point about *acceptance*. And now she's not even willing to hear me. She'd rather see me called brain damaged than face what I'm sure is out there."

"Let me get an ice pack," Mildred says, eying his knee, as he unknowingly tries to stretch it. "Or maybe a heating pad?"

"No, please. I'm fine. Really."

"So what can I do? Tell me what I can do."

"Go to New York," he says definitively, looking up. His right hand reaches down and covers his knee like a dome. Not touching it, but sheltering it for warmth. "Go to New York for me."

Lucy
Fall 2015

EDITH FRANKS CALLS it insubordination. She says there are procedures and chain of command, and that people cannot just come and go as they please. She emphasizes that she is not insensitive to the situation, but that these rules are in place in order to *protect* people who may find themselves in unfortunate situations. It is to their benefit to follow the rules. That's how the system is designed, and to benefit from the system, one has to follow the guidelines of that system. Otherwise, Edith Franks says, it simply is insubordination.

Throughout the morning, it all gets relayed to Lucy from Sarina. Mostly through emails and texts. Finally, Lucy calls Sarina to tell Sarina that she shouldn't put herself in the middle. Not to jeopardize her own job over this. It's meant to be a quick call. To put this line to rest. Sarina hardly listens. She starts right in, saying Edith Franks is out of her mind about this. That Edith Franks herself has become a little derelict in her duties at the Archives, instead solely focused on drafting a memo and scheduling meetings with superiors about how Lucy cannot just *not* come to work without having filed the proper requests, had them approved, and then confirm the potential return date. "At the very least," Edith told Sarina, "she'd better come in with a doctor's note." And when Sarina reminded Edith Franks that this wasn't an issue of illness, all Edith could respond with was, "Well, she'll need some kind of note. People can't just determine their own absences." And with the relay of information, Lucy feels a little bad for trying to rush Sarina off the call. She sees her co-worker sticking up for her. Being an ally. But she knows the slightest opening will turn to the latest on Henry, and at four hours out since the news reached her, and one since the explosives went off, there is no information yet, as the rubble still is being searched, the smoke literally being cleared, and the FBI and bomb experts and rescue workers are cluttering the surrounding and immediate areas with everyone seeking clues and information, while casualties are trapped and lost under the concrete. She just can't get into it with Sarina. With anyone. She can only hide under the covers, watch the cable news' ongoing coverage, and keep an eye on her phone for Henry's number.

Yet he hasn't phoned.

It is only Edith Franks who keeps calling. Edith Franks who has upped the frequency from once in the first hour to twice by eleven, to four times just before noon. Lucy has let them stack up, one after the other, and when she glances at the voicemail list on her phone, she is beginning to see a mountain of Ediths. And though she wants to delete them instantly, Lucy can't quite bring herself to do it. Partly because she still has an innate fear of Edith Franks and her authority. But mostly she does not want to change anything that has been laid out before her, afraid that any intervention on her part could affect the natural plan of the world that will lead her back to Henry.

On the TV, a reporter on site, which actually is about five blocks away and behind a police barricade, says that since the bombs exploded last hour, the local FBI and the sheriff's office have given a hotline phone number for relatives to call who suspect someone missing or injured. The reporter looks like she is local to the area, called into action by the national network. She has a youthful face with cheeks that still slightly bubble, and unusually large doe eyes that she tightens and narrows to cue the gravity of the situation. Behind her rise plumes of gray smoke. She might as well be in front of a nineteenth-century factory. The reporter repeats the hotline information, and as the shot cuts back to the view from the circling helicopter, the number runs along the bottom border of the screen.

Lucy stares at the number for a moment, just watching it as though she might absorb it. Then, coming to, she picks up her phone and opens the memos app. She types *Hot Line*. Then she moves the cursor between the two words and deletes the space.

Two digits at a time, she slowly pecks in the phone number, distant, doing it as though it were for someone else. Lucy can't imagine calling. She can't imagine really needing to call. Instead, she imagines herself as the conscientious friend whose most notable trait is her thoughtfulness.

Just as she is about to write down the final two numbers, she looks up to see the shot cut to a commercial. For some drug. A woman in a rolling meadow with animated magnetic waves radiating and bouncing off her head.

The phone rings again, and again it is Edith Franks.

Edith Franks will ride it out. She will not hang up when it becomes clear that Lucy will not answer. She will hang onto every possible ring, so determined, and will leave yet another message, making sure to get the last word in.

·

Was there a clue? Some piece of intuition? Even a sense that something might go wrong? A parting *I love you* before the flight out that reeked of an odd finality? Any preclusion?

The foreshadowing is always supposed to be there. Sometimes you sense it in the moment, and most times you recognize it in hindsight.

But there they are over the weekend. There they are together just yesterday afternoon. And Henry, two years older than her at twenty-five, standing in the sand with dark Ray-Bans on, head turned like he's posed and contemplating the vast Pacific, when in fact he is turning from the sun. Henry, who'd managed to convince his college sweetheart to marry him as soon as she graduated. Henry, who works in his first career job and delivers an ambitious enthusiasm, the kind of passion his boss says comes with youth, and that combining his new experiences with the fire in the belly will take him places. Henry, who stands over six feet, average features at first glance until he smiles, at which point his cheekbones emerge and his teeth radiate, like that cartoon librarian shedding her glasses and removing the pins from her hair. Henry who has crossed over from the still-filling-out teenage body of most college boys into the peak solid stature of a man.

29

When Lucy looks at him watching the ocean, the way the light is hitting him, making an awkward shadow, like boys pointing flashlights under their chins in bathroom mirrors, she sees Henry first in middle age, and then in old age. She sees a distinguished ruddiness about him, a battler who has warded off failure. Even picturing him in his old age, she envisions an eager kindness, not content to settle into the world, teaching their children and grandchildren to carry on an ethic of productivity in whatever they choose to do. And when Henry turns to catch her staring, quickly she averts her glance, convinced her thoughts play across her face as though they are projected on a movie screen. It is then when she sees his shadow roll over the sand, and in direct contrast to everything she's just observed, it is one of a child—short, awkward posture, and arms that hang, not quite helpless, but unsure of their full purpose and potential.

Could that have been the moment?

Replaying every angle of their parting hour reveals nothing. She had a 4:50 flight, and there'd been some confusion about the hotel shuttle, so she ended up in a taxi with a little less comfort time than she preferred, despite the concierge and the driver assuring her there would be time to spare. (Have they not been in a TSA line these days?) Henry had walked her down to the lobby, carrying her tote, and he had on jeans and a dark blue polo shirt and flips-flops that flapped behind him as they walked. He had overcompensated calmness in light of her stress about getting to the airport on time, something she recognized instantly by the way he slowed his speech, talked a little more breathily, and punctuated his sentences with a smile. It rarely worked on her; she knew the tactic. While they waited out front, Henry made a point of saying to call him as soon as she heard from Dr. Shore tomorrow. No matter what time of day. No matter when. Never mind his schedule. Just call him. And she'd nodded, looking at the concierge, then up the street to see if the cab was coming. When finally it arrived, she slid into the back. Holding on to the top of the open door, Henry handed her her tote. He said to remember to call after Dr. Shore called, and then as he closed the door, his final words were, "Have a safe flight," to which she reflexively and nonsensically replied, "You too."

Maybe that was the moment?

•

Private Caller. She hesitates. A 50-50 chance. In a way she hopes it is Sarina because she doesn't want to explain to Dr. Shore what she already knows about not being pregnant. No matter what, nothing ever is out in the world without first being spoken.

It is Sarina. And Sarina is whispering. There is a slight echo that Sarina apologizes for, explaining that she's calling from the corner in the foyer, kitty-corner from the gift shop. She says, "If Edith knew I had you on the line, I swear she'd crawl right into my phone, slither her way through the airwaves and come out through yours."

The image makes Lucy smile. But it also sends a shiver. Maybe because she can actually picture it happening. "Thanks for taking the brunt," she says to

Sarina. Her eyes are glued to the television. It's the same perspective from the helicopter, circling and circling and circling.

Sarina's voice lowers. "Any news?"

"I just keep watching the TV."

"I've been reading about explosions."

"It all looks really chaotic."

"Have you called the police? The FBI or something? To let them know?"

"There are tens of thousands of people who are in that area." The screen cuts to the young reporter several blocks away. Again, the hotline flashes. Again, Lucy forgets to note the last two numbers. Quickly the broadcast returns to the aerial view.

"You could just let them know. Maybe they could get in touch with Henry there, and reassure you that everything is fine."

"I appreciate you calling." It is strange that Sarina, a randomly placed cubicle neighbor at the State Archives, is her one lifeline right now.

"Would you like me to call? I can call, if you'd like."

Lucy hears the buzzing of an incoming call. Her shoulders tense. Part of her is afraid to look. She says to hold on. She holds the phone away and glances just enough at the screen to see it's not Henry. Back to Sarina she says, "It's just Edith Franks." The buzzing continues, and it will continue until Edith leaves a message. "Maybe keep talking a little bit more. A little bit longer."

The phone slips partway down her ear. She's barely listening to Sarina filling time with a story about a missing file. The chopper camera is zooming in on what appears to be the heart of the attack. It is pure demolition. A landscape of busted concrete, random girders, and broken glass, all formed into a relief map of peaks and valleys. And when she hears the final vibration, a more pronounced one, she knows that Edith Franks has said her piece. Cutting Sarina off, Lucy says she needs to go.

Sarina asks if she should call on Lucy's behalf.

"Tens of thousands of people," Lucy says. "There are tens of thousands of people."

The coverage cuts to another story, and so Lucy races through the channels, past the game shows and the soap operas and the talk shows and the infomercials and the dancing puppets until she settles on CNN. She recognizes the scene by the same camera angles from above. A voiceover says they will be staying with it all day. At least she can count on the company.

Nothing has changed. There are no updates. A few witnesses who describe the explosion. Rumors of a forthcoming statement from the local sheriff. And there is confirmation that the local FBI is leading the beginning of the investigation, which one of the commentators says is a *very strong* suggestion that terrorism is suspected.

There is no information on victims, other than a reporter saying into a windblown microphone that he's been told to expect "mass casualties, including loss of life." He notes that family members have begun arriving, and are gathering behind the police lines. Waiting. Trying to phone. A lot of hugging. Flowers and bouquets. Cards and notes. One woman, a mother of two, grandmother of three, earlier showed the reporter a text from her husband who works in food

services at the building; it read, *Don't worry. Smoky but I.*
The reporter makes clear to the viewing audience that
he cannot verify the date and time of the text, nor can
he confirm the husband and his employment in food
services in the building. "Still," he says, before throwing
it back to the desk, "standing here it is impossible not to
feel the fear and anguish."

At the news desk, the anchor says, "I guess we'll
have to wait. Perhaps we'll learn more from the press
conference . . . Now let's take another look from the
sky."

Lucy feels herself lifting, as though she is the
bird who will give the bird's-eye view. Down below it
looks smokier. More littered. The police presence is
more visible, and tucked into the corner of the screen
is a separate feed of small police brigades patrolling
neighborhood streets, rifles in hand, looking in car
windows, knocking on doors. Residents can be seen
in their backyards. One, a small boy, is looking up and
waving at a helicopter. Lucy leans forward, squinting and
trying to magnify the TV screen. From all angles, her
attention has turned to the bystanders. She is trying to
catch a glimpse of Henry. At this point, the boundaries
have changed: just a glimpse would suffice in place of
a phone call.

Sarina is right—she probably should phone in her
concern to the hotline. At least give them her name and
her contact information. But it seems so random. Out
of the zillions of people in the area, why would she
presume Henry to be part of this? Is it just because he is
at a conference and giving a training? Surely throughout
the area hotels there are meeting rooms named Sequoia,

Manzanita, Pacific, Executive, Coastal, Governor's, Presidio, Del Mar, Bayside, Vista del Monte, Laguna, Yerba Buena, Regency, Mission, Thousand Cranes, Redondo, Valley, Golden Gate, and Orchard, rooms filled with conference attendees being presented everything from new research in renal therapy to utilizing your POS system. The odds of Henry being among the rubble are infinitesimal. Like those comparisons they make about the odds of being in a plane crash versus winning the lotto.

Yes, Sarina is right—Lucy really should phone her concern to the hotline. At leastles give them her name and her contact information. Just in case. But she is afraid. She is afraid of stirring something up. Afraid of adding Henry into a mix where he hadn't been before, as if that simple, prudent task might ensure his fate. Afraid that saying it aloud will thrust her out of the *before* and knee-deep into the *after*. It is the same reason she hasn't called her parents in North Carolina or Henry's parents in Maryland. Neither have yet made the connection that the bombing and shooting rampage has taken place in the same city where Lucy and Henry spent the weekend, and where Henry remained for work. And Lucy will not bring that to their attention. It's enough that Sarina is thinking that way. The fewer people who are worried or panicked or nervous or afraid, the better for Henry. It's like a Ouija board, she thinks; where the collective energy can cause the planchette to glide all the way across the board, away from its intended destination.

On the bottom of the screen is a crawler that reads that the president will be making a statement within the next hour. She remembers that following tragedies, the president often calls the families. Wouldn't that be something?

•

Edith Franks would be right to label it insubordination. Edith Franks would be right to cite chain of command. Edith Franks would be right to refer to terms in the employee handbook. And she would even be presenting a logical and cohesive argument that Lucy is not coming into work purely on the possibility that something could be wrong, a possibility dictated by an accumulation of a series of circumstances—one that any number of people up and down the coast could be finding in their own lives. Edith Franks would be right. But does that mean she has to call every goddamn five minutes?

•

Here is what she thinks: Her stomach is growling, but she is not hungry. Her head is pounding and banging and stuck in drive, but it does not hurt. Her breathing feels like it has no ability or capacity to take in oxygen, but she is full of life. Her eyes are laser-focused on the television, picking up every nuance, every detail, registering every fact, every word, but she feels blind. And though she is wrapped in her red terry cloth robe, nestled under a top sheet that is at least a three-hundred count, two cotton blankets, and a middle-weight comforter with spots of roses, she still is cold. Especially her feet.

To make its cocoon, a caterpillar secretes silk through its mouth, and then slowly wraps the silk around the body, sealing and protecting the insect from the outside world. But initially, because it is silk, the cocoon is soft. It is fragile. Contact with air is what hardens it into more of a shell—the armor that will protect it until the caterpillar is ready to assume its adult form.

Although Lucy is wrapped, kind of protected, she is aware that it is so fragile. And she also is aware of the effect of coming into contact with the outside world. Aware that it could harden her into an armor that she will never outlive.

It is best not to go out.

It is best to avoid contact.

It is best to be quarantined.

At least for now.

That is what she thinks.

•

Nothing has changed on the television coverage. And with no changes, and with no word from Henry, the remote possibilities start to feel more like tangible actualities.

The hotline number flashes on the screen. This time, Lucy only looks at the last two numbers. Instead of her phone, she reaches into her nightstand drawer for a pen, and without looking, she writes the last two digits on the back of a magazine, the one white space in an otherwise dark and shadowed cognac ad. When Sarina urged her to call, it had been a maybe. A we'll-see. Now it is just a matter of when. Something like that takes strength. The phone can weigh a ton.

Once again, Edith rings. Lucy just stares at the face

of her mobile phone, seeing Edith's name and number soundtracked by quarter-note vibrations. When it stops, in the space before yet another Edith Franks voicemail will announce itself, Lucy says aloud, "Edith, I love you too." But she isn't being ironic. Nor is she being sarcastic.

Edgar
Fall 1993

MRS. DUNCAN ASKS if she'll have to go the police. She asks if she'll have to go to court to enforce the order. Mrs. Duncan is exasperated, and she is tired of yelling at her son by phone, in as much as being firm and reaching her boiling point is yelling. Mrs. Duncan is beyond reminding Edgar that she still has power of attorney over his healthcare, and as long as the cognitive issues continue she has every plan to execute that power, with the first order of business being a follow up visit with Dr. Merman. And she swears by god that she'll have Pastor and the local police cart off Edgar in handcuffs and a straightjacket if that's what it takes.

He repeats he is not having any cognitive dysfunction. None of the so-called confabulation.

She says, "The very fact you say that is further proof that you need to see Dr. Merman."

He remains silent long enough to hear his mother say, "Well, I guess this call is over." It's his way of hanging up on her.

Edgar limps back to the couch, picking up his cane off the floor midway back. It had slipped out of his hand and been kicked to the side when he stood quickly to get to the phone. He'd been hoping it was Mildred. He hasn't heard from her since last Friday, when he'd suggested that on his behalf she go to New York to look for his sister. Since the beating, she typically checked in on him at least twice during the week. Always he told her not to bother. Now it turns out she should bother. A week has passed, and he's felt trapped between the days. Disconnected. He needs something to counteract the incessant brainwashing of his mother, who is so unwilling to deal with the reality that Erin might be out there that she'll make up her own narrative and cast him as the bewildered villain.

Mildred does ground him. That, mother, is a truth anyone can see.

As the day comes to an end, he waits by the window, relaxed by his cigarette, looking out to see if she'll come after work, as usual and with her, in hand, the Friday Zelda's pizza.

•

Over the past week, Edgar has made phone calls. Starting in lower Manhattan, closest to the Trade Towers, he's called New York Presbyterian Hospital. Bellevue. Mount Sinai Beth Israel. He's moved gradually though midtown to uptown. Roosevelt Hospital. The Cornell Medical Center. The Columbia Medical Center. Each time, he starts with his sister's name—just in case. And then he moves to Jane Doe. Each time he is told that they cannot release such information. He asks, "What if I describe her? Tell you her age?" They say they are sorry. Frustrated the same way on each and every phone call, he says, "Does the bureaucracy really trump the possibility that my sister might be in a coma or worse? Can't someone at least just look to see if there is anybody who even resembles her?" Each time he is told he should call the police. They are the ones who investigate and follow through on these matters. Each time, he hangs up. What he doesn't say is that he can't call the police. He'd been told over and over by them after Erin's initial disappearance that with no evidence of foul play, no motive, no anything, there is nothing to investigate. They'd told him that people over the age of eighteen have a right to disappear. They have a right to want to be alone. But he'd kept calling. Pleading. Demanding. Each time, his complaint was entered into the police system. Finally, the detective who Edgar reached out to over and over told Edgar to stop calling until there was some concrete evidence of something. A letter. A threat. Drained bank accounts. That kind of thing. And when Edgar protested, saying that the fact she'd disappeared meant that *all* traces of her had disappeared, and why can't the NYPD just do its job, the detective said that the next time Edgar made one of these calls, he was going to issue a warrant for Edgar's arrest for interfering in a case—*every single goddamn one we are working on*! So no, hospital administrator. No, nursing desk. No, Patient Care rep. He cannot call the police.

•

Something is different tonight. Usually when Mildred comes over with the pizza, they both sit in the living room—Edgar on the couch, Mildred in one of the matching chairs. They'll eat off the glass coffee table. Chat for a while. And when the plates are lifted, the drinks taken away, and the little moisture rings that were left behind start to clear, it's the sign that the evening is ending.

Tonight, while Edgar has his usual spot on the couch, Mildred is sitting at the dining table. For all intents and purposes, she would be in another room if the pocket-doors still worked. Her chair is turned so that she half-faces him. The napkin under her soda can sticks to the bottom when she lifts it. Like pulling up all the roots.

Edgar was relieved when she'd shown up. Mildred had knocked on the door at 5:15, much earlier than normal, and then entered with the pizza. She said she'd left work around four because she'd have to leave here a little earlier than normal. Still, she wanted to make sure they had their time together. There was a plan she'd made, she said. She'd forgotten until this morning. It was made a while ago. Long before this was the regular arrangement.

He told her it was okay; he said he understood and he just was glad to see her. She nodded, started to say something, but instead turned, disappearing off to the kitchen for plates.

Something is different tonight. Mildred looks distracted. She keeps bringing up little anecdotes about work at the social services agency, talking about people Edgar hardly knows. She says how a voicemail exchange that had concluded with *All right, then* had turned into three people not speaking, two of them convinced that it had been a passive-aggressive put down, while the other one was offended that her attempt at being agreeable had been taken as just the opposite. Mildred spoke about how the Executive Director said that in order to run leaner everyone needed to cut back on *paper copies*, even though the memo had been printed on paper and stuffed in all the mailboxes, with extras left by the copier machine. And she told him about how a client had come in seeking services and it turned out she was faking her situation, and that in fact she was very well off (she even had a lot of investments in the stock market) but she was too cheap to pay for job search services out of her own pocket. "And that," Mildred says, "was just Monday."

He doesn't know whether or not she's about to leap into Tuesday, but he jumps in. Cuts her off. It's something he needs to say. The unspoken needs to be said. He says, "You don't have to go to New York for me."

She takes a bite from the edge of the pizza slice. Then in toward the middle. She swats down a small thread of cheese that settles on her chin. "I know," she says, shaking the string off the side of her hand. "I know."

•

On Sunday morning, two days later, Mildred shows up unexpectedly at the apartment. In the doorway, she stands with a pink pastry box. A thin string is wrapped around it, fraying at the tight knot on the box's top. She never arrives empty-handed. She once said it was how she'd been raised. It's easy to make a bad reputation, but almost impossible to shed it.

Edgar invites her in, a little perplexed. He can't ever remember seeing her on a weekend. In truth, he'd only known her fleetingly while volunteering with her at the social service agency, and if he hadn't found himself with her on that fateful day at the Capitol and thus intertwined in the aftermath, he is sure their connection never would have been anything other than a passing, polite hello.

Her feet dance a little in place. Eyes dart around the room. "It's really nice outside," she says. "Really nice." She puts the pink pastry box down on the dining room table and walks to the window, pushing the drapes a little more to each side. The room turns a little brighter. As if someone inched up a dimmer switch.

Edgar says it looks breezy.

"The cool air is burning off rapidly." She sounds like a weather report. "Something about high pressure systems."

He asks what she brought, and she says *Oh, yeah*, like she forgot she even came with anything. "A few pastries," she says. "You know, croissants, scones. Morning things."

What is she doing here?

Mildred starts to untie the string. Her fingers are slim. Delicate. It's easy to imagine them sliding between the loops and elbows that bind the knot. But she can't loosen it. So she pulls up on the thread, hoping to snap it, and it plays like an out-of-tune B string. "Damnit," she mutters, and then pushes the whole box away as though it is part of a conspiracy.

Edgar limps in, holding a pair of scissors against the handle of his cane. "Try this," he says. He's unaccustomed to seeing her rattled.

She says, "I don't know who they think can open these things."

He hands the scissors to her. "Here you go."

"Please," she says. "Go ahead." She pulls up the string, stretching it into a taut peak, while steadying the box against the table. "Cut," she commands. "Cut it now."

Edgar ambles in closer. It is hard for him to find his balance. All movement feels a little wobbly. A month or so ago he might have said something, but now he keeps it to himself, especially since people such as his mother, Pastor, and Dr. Merman have tried to paint him as being deformed in one way or another. He feels his hip trembling, as though the muscles are over-taxed and on the verge of breaking. Brandishing the scissors, he reaches around her, conceding all his balance to the cane. He angles the upper and lower blades around the string and cuts down. His knee begins trembling, like they're calling timber, and he reaches his hands out, but can't quite grab the table. It is a slow-motion fall backward, one that feels like it has all the time in the world. He drops the scissors, which thud on the edge of the table, and just as his cane is about to slip out, Mildred's hands clamp around his upper arm and on the small of his back, steadying him until he can balance.

At the same time, they look at the table. The dropped scissors have scarred the corner of the table. An indention has broken the veneer, exposing the raw wood.

Neither says anything.

Like a jack in the box, the pink lid pops open on its own.

Edgar is so preoccupied with why Mildred has shown up on a Sunday that he forgets to eat. On his plate is a croissant, golden and flaky, with an end torn off. Everything she's said has sounded like a prelude to something else, yet she has yet to make any transition.

She hasn't touched her scone. Once or twice she's blown across the surface of her coffee. But she hasn't taken a sip.

He says, "I decided not to say anything on Friday. I didn't want you to take it the wrong way."

She asks, "Take what the wrong way?"

He says, "I haven't said."

Mildred smiles. "A reasonable person might suggest that I must have already taken it the wrong way."

He tries to match her smile. He even tries to laugh. But somewhere between Erin's disappearance and the beating, he's found it nearly impossible to express any kind of humor. Like that area of his brain was the damaged part.

"Tell me," she says. "Tell me what you meant to say."

Edgar reaches down and tears off the other end of the pastry. Still looking down at his plate, he says, "I spent the whole week calling."

"Calling?"

"Hospitals." He reaches for a napkin. His fingers still feel coated in butter.

"For . . .?"

He can read her concern; that she is afraid of where this might be heading. Quickly, he shifts to stave that off. Put her at ease. "It was nothing I ever expected of you," he assures. "I wasn't calling because I planned that you'd be going. None of it was done with you in mind."

Mildred cocks her head. Her eyes narrow. Part of

Edgar hates when she gets that expression because it makes her look so much like his sister. It spooks him. Plus, with Erin that expression usually presaged a comment that pointed out some stupidity on his part. Mildred clarifies, "You mean you called hospitals in New York?"

"Where else would I call a hospital?"

She doesn't answer.

He says, "She's not in any of them. There is no one with her name in any one of the area wards." He drags his finger over the groove the falling scissor made.

Mildred lets out a deep sigh. It is one of great relief, a sigh so bottled up and pronounced that it strikes Edgar as odd. "That must be a real comfort," she says. "A real comfort. I know this possibility of the Trade Towers has been on your mind the past few weeks."

Elbows on the table, he leans forward to her. His bad knee straightens out to the side. He's so close to her, he can feel the heat coming off the surface of her coffee. His head is shaking. "That's not taking into account Jane Does," he explains, conscious of bringing empathy to each word. He hates to ruin it for Mildred, but he also has to be truthful and realistic. "She could still be in the hospital. Or they could have released her, without knowing her name. No one will tell me. They say it's a police matter, but the New York police have long made clear that they aren't interested in anything to do with my sister."

Mildred pulls back a little. Her arms fold over her midsection. "Are you saying that after those calls you still believe Erin's disappearance is due to the World Trade Tower explosion?"

"*Believe?*" He shrugs. "It's not really about *belief.* You know that better than anybody."

Mildred reaches to the center of the table, and pushes on the lid of the pink pastry box. With her index finger, she runs the tip around the edges, pressing down as she moves her finger, slowly sealing the top. Her eyes glaze into a middle distance. She says, "There is something I need to talk you about." To Edgar it is a sentence that takes a half-hour to be said, with each word slowed down to a warped wave, every syllable taking its time in a slow gush that fills up and floods the room before the next one comes.

•

Mrs. Duncan has no interest in hearing it. Mrs. Duncan says it is the least of her concerns what he thinks about what she does or does not tell his friends. Mrs. Duncan says that it is his health and well-being that is her chief concern, not whether or not she embarrasses him. And when he asks how she even knows Mildred, Mrs. Duncan says there were many tense moments in the hospital following the attack. Plus, there were many lulls. He starts to protest, but Mrs. Duncan has no interest in hearing it. Mrs. Duncan says she for one is glad the girl had the courage to go through with it, because you, Edgar, are listening to no one. Mrs. Duncan wants her son to know that she expects him to go through with Mildred's offer, and as soon as they hang up, she expects Edgar to pick up the phone promptly, dial Mildred's house, and first tell her he is sorry for being so rude and for insisting she leave this morning, especially when he knows she was only expressing her concern; and when Mildred accepts the apology, Edgar is to say he will accept her offer to take him next week for the treatments Dr. Merman has recommended. Mrs. Duncan has no interest in hearing any different. She is too impatient to wait for cues or silence. Mrs. Duncan says, "Well, I guess this call is over." And then she hangs up. She doesn't even hear him agree. Mrs. Duncan has no need to, she knew what his answer would be well before he knew it.

•

Edgar won't see Mildred again. At least not until more than a quarter century has past, and even then it will be on a sidewalk, at a busy crossing on L Street, ironically kitty-corner to the end of the Capitol lawn where the attack took place. And she'll only look half-familiar at first take. She will stand with a recognizable grace, one hand clutching a phone, and the other dug deep inside her jacket pocket. She will look official, as though her nonprofit days have long ago been traded up for something that resembles lobbyist or chief-of-staff. Her shoulders will be pushed up, as though shielding her from the early spring breeze. In some respects, she will look exactly the same as she did when he knew her, but it is the twenty-plus years of time that will make him doubt himself. Her hair will be much lighter, cut into a mid-length bob that just reaches the back of her neck. Her face will be a little thinner, making a slight shadow in her cheeks that accents and defines the precision of her bone structure, with lips pronounced by a brick red lipstick that stand apart from her somewhat translucent skin. Her eyes will still pierce, yet when she narrows them in response to a blast of wind, Edgar will see the lines arc downward, oddly shiny. Though her clothes still hang off her as though precisely placed on a mannequin by a window dresser, she will look a little larger in stature, as though she commands that much more space on the Earth. And he will look at her, and she will have no idea he is watching. She might not recognize him, now that he no longer walks with a cane. His hair will have turned almost fully gray, his face longer and more drawn, but his presence much more commanding and confident, grown used to power and control from running and growing Duncan Distributors. She will glance once toward him, a slightly bewildered look on her face, as though sensing something familiar or forgotten is nearby. But Edgar won't say anything. When the light turns, she will cross ahead of the pack, making a beeline for the Capitol entrance. Instead of crossing, he will round the corner, and then walk uptown another two blocks before crossing L Street. He is taking no chances.

Crossing the street alone, he glances right, in the direction of the Capitol. He can only see the gold-leafed dome towering out through the trees. And it makes him think of the last time he'd seen Mildred, in front of the inpatient rehab center up in El Dorado Hills, when she'd dropped him off on a Monday morning, telling him that whether it took three weeks or thirty weeks, that she would proudly pick him up when it ended. He couldn't even look at her, an agent of his family. He'd gotten out and shut the door without saying a word. A cold morning, yet the outlines of his face felt warmed and defined. With the sunlight bursting against the window, it made it impossible to see into the car. He didn't turn around when she drove off, although sometimes in his dreams he hears the tires grinding against the gravel on the road, fading away but with the sound never really gone.

At the Cognitive Rehab center, Edgar worked on strategies to better access his memories; to find techniques to recognize the tendencies toward confabulation. The staff believed his condition wasn't a physiological result from the strike to the head, but rather a psychological consequence of the beating, one in which his brain reordered and reinterpreted memories, particularly those pertaining to traumatic events (such as the attack, Erin's disappearance, and his father's early death), all in service of trying to realign his psychological state to one not flailing in chaos and confusion, but rather one in which a positive and logical order guided him. He worked with groups. He worked individually. He did brain exercises. Wrote in journals. And halfway through he even agreed it would be best for him to take over the family business at the end of the treatment. Sitting on a bench outside with a therapist named Patricia, he suggested that it was time for his obsession with Erin's disappearance to end. He wasn't looking at Patricia when he spoke. His gaze was set on the valley below them, surrounded by golden hills of dried and dying grasses. All the way across the horizon was a blackened knoll, scorched by fire nearly a season ago. He said, "I realize I am making it be a part of everything I see."

"You understand how it has infiltrated your memories?"

He tapped his index finger against his right temple.

"Sometimes there is little that is rational in here."

Patricia said his progress was outstanding. She said she thought he was about ready to take on the business of living out in the world again.

He said, "Who would want to just sit back and watch it spin?"

On the day he was discharged, Edgar stood at the entrance with his single suitcase. It felt lighter than when he'd entered. He'd spoken to no one on the way out, only giving Patricia a little smile that for some reason seemed to disarm her. Maybe it was a balance shifting? He lifted his bag into the bed of Pastor's waiting pick-up, and then slid into the cab, pulling his cane in behind him. "Seat belt," Pastor said. And nothing else was said as they wove out of the driveway and down the hill to Interstate 99.

Through the open window, the air was fresh, then smoky, then fresh again. Pastor had the radio on. It was oldies, but not the kind of oldies Edgar knew. These were filled with strings and nasally female singers. About halfway back, Pastor asked, "So, are you all fixed now?"

Edgar nodded, watching the road in front of them. "I got a few things settled."

"Well, you seem to be walking better, at least."

As they neared his house, coming up H Street, it seemed like a whole season had passed since he'd left. The leaves were budding and green. The light made people on the sidewalk look present and alive, in some sort of shared communion, as opposed to the shadow figures drifting through the fog that he'd remembered from before. When Pastor pulled up in front of Edgar's apartment, even the building looked different, as though its façade had been repainted and then shined.

Pastor didn't cut the engine. He undid his seatbelt, and without turning down the radio, he said, "I can help you up with your bag."

"I got it." Edgar shook him off. "I can manage."

Pastor put his hands on the wheel. "I guess they did fix you there, didn't they?"

Edgar opened the door, and leading with his cane, he slid down onto the street. His hand gripped the doorframe for balance.

Pastor said, "Seven-thirty too early tomorrow?"

"I'll be ready."

"Your first week, and my last one."

"I'll be waiting downstairs."

"Don't forget your bag. In the back."

"I got it."

"You sure you don't need a hand?"

"I got it."

"That place back there," Pastor said, shaking his head, "it's like a miracle farm."

Inside, his apartment was just as it had been the morning Mildred drove him up to the center. It had been spotless when he left, and somehow even more spotless when he returned. He'd made her cart away the one remaining Zelda's box; in retrospect, it was less about the mess, but rather about already eliminating all traces of Mildred.

The sunlight coming through the windows made the white furniture even whiter, and the room even larger. Here he was, twice removed. This space had housed him before the accident, been turned into a kind of holding cell afterward, and now it felt like a home again.

Last night before leaving the rehab center, the staff had given him a farewell with slices of white frosted cake for everyone. They'd said pretty much what Pastor had said, how well fixed he was. They'd raised their forks, toasting Edgar, congratulating themselves, and wishing him well as he entered the next phase of his life, a healthy mind who'd be taking over the family business. When they'd demanded he say something, he'd said, "I couldn't have made such a big change without all of you." They raised their forks again. Then they left him with a sheet of paper that outlined generalized strategies for how to cope with any of those false memories that might come back under stressful circumstances. He'd said he couldn't imagine needing it in the future; one thing lost to his memory was the concept of stress. Everybody had laughed. Then they reminded him he'd agreed to regularly attend families-of-victims support meetings. Even when he felt fine, it was good preventative medicine. Plus, unsaid in this semi-public forum, it was a condition of his mother's, lest she have him remanded back for treatment should there be any indication he was regressing. And Mrs. Duncan would be vigilant.

He leaves his bag in the hallway, near the bedroom. He goes straight to the dining room table, the same chair where Mildred had sat distanced on the Friday night she'd come to betray him as an agent of his mother's, and later that following Sunday morning when she returned, knowing she had to go through with the plan.

There is no time for eating. No time for a drink of water.

He reaches for the phone book, and then the phone. Opening the book, he takes out a sheet of handwritten numbers. He dials the first one, asking for patient services. His finger rubs back and forth over the scissors wound that's left a divot on the table. Although almost anything can be fixed, this one seems irreparable. After a brief wait, a woman comes on the other end. She says, "New York Presbyterian Hospital."

He says, "My name is Edgar Duncan. I have reason to believe that several months ago, my sister, Erin, was seriously injured in the bombing of World Trade Center, and that she may have been brought to your hospital."

Lucy
Fall 2015

SHE WAS TOO young to really understand 9/11. What Lucy most remembers is that she was nine, about to turn ten on September 12, and that when her birthday came the day after the airplanes, she sat slumped in a blue Adirondack chair on a wraparound porch with several families from the neighborhood in Trinity Park in Durham, North Carolina, just blocks east of Duke's freshman campus, where her father still works as an administrator. The Wilsons hosted the dinner, one of the few couples with whom her parents were friends. The rest of the guests were people they knew casually—social gatherings, the aisles of the grocery stores, readings at the Regulator. It would have been odd to have predicted such an occasion. But after two days of being glued to the television and to the radio, in the late afternoon after the airplanes and the day of Lucy's ninth birthday, the Wilsons phoned around inviting friends for an ad hoc dinner, instinctively understanding the need for community. Each family hastily converted what they'd planned to cook for dinner in their own homes into covered pots and Pyrex dishes. Lucy's parents brought the birthday cake they'd intended for her, a double layer of chocolate sheet cake that her mother was mortaring with white frosting in the minutes before they were about to walk down to the

Wilsons, chanting that they had to get going, they'd be the last ones there.

On the short trek from her house to the Wilsons, Lucy remembers everything being still. Although it normally was a quiet neighborhood, tonight it felt like the volume had been turned off. She and her parents walked in a single line down the block. Her mother carried the cake, while she and her father held steel pots with lids that bounced like hi-hats with every step. Approaching the Wilson's house, hearing low voices coming off the front porch, she imagined the unspoken dread of a lost explorer stumbling back into civilization.

Lucy remembers some of the adults talked about contingency plans in case the next attack happened here. Mr. Wilson spoke of war, although from the way his face balled up, it was hard to tell if he was for it or worried about it. There were other children there. The Wilsons had a boy and girl one year apart—one in preschool and one in half-day kindergarten. The Pollocks from up the street had two girls roughly the same age, while the Jeffersons had a baby boy fast asleep in the upstairs bedroom. The kids stayed inside, in the family room, playing with cars and blocks in front of a television set with a video of a Muppets movie for background music.

She was too young to really understand 9/11. But what Lucy does remember she remembers from that night on the porch, the day after—her birthday. She remembers running her palm back and forth in one place on the chair's armrest and feeling a bubble of flaking paint. She remembers secretly picking at it, the casual but deliberate machinery of her thumb and forefinger, just as she had when she'd once picked at a scab on her leg against her mother's admonitions. And she remembers the moment when her mother looked up, first at her father, and then at the rest of the table, looking ghostly and brave. She looked like someone who three hours into a drive suddenly realized she had left the oven on. And Lucy remembers seeing her mouthing something at her father, and then with a silent count-off the two of them begin singing *Happy Birthday*, and at first it is just the two of them, but soon the rest of the table joins in, then the children's voices join from faraway inside the house, and by time the tempo shifts to the slow largo at the end she hears her father trying to harmonize, and she recognizes the notes from all the other times she's heard the song and from her own eking out of them when she's bowed the tune on her ¾ cello in front of her teacher, but she also recognizes how flat he sounds, as though what he hears in his head is not quite what is able to come through the rest of the body.

As the voices fade, and the crickets start to stir, there is a low wind that blows along the porch, bending the candle flames, and lifting up the ends of the red vinyl table cloth; with its floral pattern there is the impression of a single rose and a single vine about to blow away. And it is warm, that wind blowing against her neck. Caressing the hair that falls without quite reaching her shoulders.

Across the street from the Wilsons is the neighborhood park, a small city park with a gazebo in the center that only was recently built though a neighborhood fundraising effort. At one of the tables inside the gazebo sits a man, alone. Lucy remembers watching him, while she continued to pick at the chip of paint. Sometimes he would gaze out at the moon. Sometimes he would bury his face in his hands. From his form, it's hard to tell who he is. It's a little unusual to see strangers in the park, especially in the gazebo, because although it is a public park, the neighborhood has made clear it is off limits to anybody whom the funding campaign wasn't meant to serve. It looks like Herman, the adult son of a never-seen elderly couple called the Jacksons, three blocks over, in a house that has grown spooked by the lack of upkeep, with a front door of flaking white paint, a side gutter dangling off the roofline, and blue-and-white striped window awnings that are faded from the sun and ripped by the wind. Lucy's parents always comment it could be a nice house. It has interesting stylings and good bones, they say. Eventually when the Jacksons pass or are too old to be on their own, someone will buy it and rehab it. But her parents take the neighborhood position in hoping that isn't Hellman; he buys the run-down homes cheap, never fixes them up, and then rents them out to noisy students whose presence only encourages the neighborhood's potential decline. But in that scenario, no one talks about Herman. It's as though he'll just go when the parents go. Often, Herman can be seen walking around the neighborhood. It's never been clear if he is just a little slow or just kind of emotionally wounded. In general, he keeps to himself. The adults always will say hello to him in an overly solicitous voice, and he'll usually look away, but, at the same time, when he is walking toward them, the adults will shift their position, walling off the children. Sometimes he walks past the park, but she's never seen him in it. But then again, maybe he only feels welcome at night? After dark?

She remembers sitting on the porch, thinking someone should invite Herman over. She remembers he glanced over in the direction of the Wilsons' house. After they acknowledged one another, Lucy remembers that she got really, really scared and only then discovered that it wasn't the dark she was afraid of, instead what can come out of it.

Lucy then remembers continuing to pick at the chip of paint until she felt it loosen, and then covering it with her hand, embarrassed, she pressed her palm down, hoping to mash it back into place.

She was too young to really understand 9/11. But Lucy remembers that birthday. She remembers the conversation. Her father's flat singing. Her mother's kiss on her cheek. And she remembers how everything felt like the last one of everything.

BOOK TWO

LUCY

WHEN THE DOUBLE doors slam at the bottom of the stairs, Amy looks up. She sits in one of the many gray folding chairs, legs crossed, facing the stage area, a yellow pad on her lap, and a pen gripped in her hand. They are in the basement of the Church of God, the COG as everyone calls it, an institution that ministers by lending space to worthy groups of people in need. On first view, having entered at the rear of the room, it matches just what Lucy had imagined: a dreary setting for a therapeutic jazz band that she was encouraged to try as an ancillary part of her counselling in the year since the attacks. Precisely what she dreaded. But taking a longer, more measured look, Lucy sees that it matches up exactly with the few aspects she hoped it might offer—it's out of the way, there's no one she knows, and it's free of expectation.

After waving Lucy up front toward the other players, Amy announces, "I think we can start now." The echo in the room makes her authority sound hollow. Amy coughs, then leans forward, her pen laser focused on the score laid out over several sheets on her music stand. With a combination of seriousness and earnestness, she amends her handwritten notes in the margins.

Although the room is sparsely populated, the sense of being watched overwhelms Lucy. After this past year, it has been hard to shake. Generally, everyone is curious. Strangers on the street. Her co-workers. Her family. The media. Even Sarina, who has become her one friend since the attacks, always is monitoring her. And when interest seems to wane, the federal prosecutors make sure she's in the news again. Her one hope for this music therapy was that it would allow her to be herself unobserved for anything other than making music. And yet right now she feels so observed.

Lucy sucks in a breath and then navigates through the lingering smell of hours-old brewed coffee, carrying her case to the front of the room, turning sideways and shimmying between a row of chairs toward the one empty seat. The bulky white plastic shell she carries bangs against her skirted thigh.

By the piano on the left side, and forming a half-circle around the woman seated on the bench, are two men with horns of varying sizes and another man with a flute. They seem to know each other. To their right, and in the back, stands the drummer, leaning over his kit and adjusting a cymbal. As the only African American among the group (something Lucy tells herself she only notices due to the context of it being a jazz combo), he seems like a ringer, perhaps a paid professional to ensure some musicality to this group of damaged amateurs.

Once up front, Lucy kneels down, partially blocked by the standup bass. It is propped up by a man about twenty years her senior; he's draped across its body, plucking an occasional string from boredom. Under the light its caramel veneer shines in streaks.

She tugs down on her skirt, sensing it is riding too high up her legs.

"We should get started now," Amy says again, straightening up and loosening her shoulders with rolling gestures. She is mousy, a little nervous by nature—so tiny that she looks like a slightly different species. Her tight-fitting clothes appear to hang like a costume, and her large silver-framed glasses look more like a disguise or mask than they do something prescriptive.

Feeling rushed, Lucy's hands shake as she opens up the cello case. It's just big enough to house a small child. A gust of wind blasts her from a circulating fan on a pole, making bearable the warm dampness of the COG basement. As she lifts the lid, Lucy is overwhelmed by nerves. Just once, she'd like something to go right, and go right on her own terms. Over the past year, her life has been one of accommodation. She has had to appease Henry's parents. Investigators. Government prosecutors. Everyone. For all of them, it seems, it's been necessary for Lucy to be in a suspended state of loss.

And so she remains.

•

In Southern California, in the jurisdiction where the shooting and bombing took place, in the ninth circuit, the U.S. Attorney's Office for the District of Southern California has been preparing its case against the one living suspect the government has in custody, Ryan Mohammad Khan, a twenty-four-year-old man currently being held at Victorville. It will not be an easy case, as there were two primary assailants who planned and executed the attack—one of them killed in a firefight with local police, and the second blown up in one of the explosions, identified only by his molars. The man in custody is trickier. Khan did not have direct involvement. He was a friend. A hanger-on. A wannabe. But there is ample evidence to show that he knew that the attack was being planned, and investigators uncovered cell phone records that suggest that he was in communication with the attackers during the assault, coaching them from his living room about the various movements of the police units, as seen on TV from the news helicopters and as reported by the various journalists. The suspect is being charged under the terrorism laws, and, by adding in a Weapons of Mass Destruction indictment, federal prosecutors will be seeking the death penalty, which, by its very fractious nature, has entered a new storyline into the conversation. And further complicating public perception is that although like the dead attackers he is American-born to East Indian parents, Ryan Mohammad Khan also served two tours in Iraq, and upon his return, it is documented that he suffered from PTSD. For the prosecution, the complicating factor about Khan's background is knowing that ending a death penalty conviction takes just one sympathetic juror. The attackers' computers showed multiple searches that indicated an allegiance to ISIS, but no such information turned up for Khan, and he has declared no such sympathies, but neither has he denied them. Legal rights advocates are calling Ryan Mohammad Khan a scapegoat. Well-known pundits, scholars, academics, and candidates in the current election cycle appear on cable news shows and talk about why this is an example of how badly the government needs a visible victory. Death penalty challengers say the government is over-reaching, and abusing its power. The feds reply by imploring the citizenry both to consider the evidence, and to think about all the people who died in the attacks.

They name them one by one. And they say to think of the children of the victims, and then to think of those who were widowed. That is where Lucy fits into their case. They need her to stanch the bleeding heart. Thus far, Lucy has declined their requests to appear on talk shows, or to give newspaper interviews. But that hasn't stopped them from invoking her in their war for public opinion. She is their star. Henry is the only remaining missing person following the explosions, and she is the embodiment of the nightmare of having to live without the closure. And lately they have been turning up the pressure on her to follow their lead on every step forward. Thus, her battle has become between her instinct for acquiescence and approval versus her need to allow herself to move into the next stage of her life. It's all on her. And yet it all feels completely out of her control.

•

Amy announces, "I want to welcome our newest members." She is looking at Lucy and the bassist. Lucy glances up, trying to pry the instrument out of the red velvet-lined case where it doesn't quite fit—one hand on the neck, while the other slips under the waist and carefully but quickly wedges the instrument upward and outward. The fan breezes by again, blowing cool air up the inside of her thigh. It feels like everyone sees the goosebumps tingling. More easily, she frees the bow from under an elastic strap. Next time she will remember to wear pants.

And then Amy, with her undergraduate degree

in Jazz Composition from Berklee, her primary instrument being the piano, but also taking several electives attached to the music therapy program; Amy who later earned an MS in clinical psychology at Cal State Fullerton, and upon completion of that became a certified bereavement counselor after an intensive week-long seminar in Sedona; Amy who only recently discovered a way to put all her interests together into a single therapy, a cocktail of all her various trainings, leans forward, traces her index finger along the first staff of the composition, her foot tapping as the last of the tuning takes places in moans and shrieks, waiting to count off the introduction to Coltrane's *Blue Train*, a cool, spooky blues in 4/4 time. "Don't worry about how it sounds," she instructs. "For now, that is." The comment brings a chuckle. "Once the groove sets in, you'll be in."

Quickly, Lucy takes her chair beside the bassist. She lays out the score on the black stand provided for her. Refines her tuning. Checks the hairs on the bow. They are too close to the bow stick; you couldn't even slide the end of a pencil under it. She knows that an over-tightened bow can alter the mechanics, rendering many of the most basic strokes impossible. Too tight, and the wood can snap. Balancing the bow on her lap, Lucy tries to turn down the tension screw. The nut barely turns. It could be from the humidity of the basement. Or it could be that it's been overly tightened for too long.

She takes in a deep breath, edges herself more into the middle of the chair, kicks her left foot forward, and balancing the instrument against her knees, she allows the body to fall back and lightly lay against her chest.

Just like she learned in her lessons as a little girl. In position, she rests her bow across the strings, and while others finish tuning, she waits endlessly for the count.

It was Lucy's regular therapist who encouraged her to contact Amy. *Playing music can be very helpful for learning to manage the daily routines of survivors of trauma. It forces us to have a constructive, focused task, but one that still needs to work together harmonically and rhythmically with others to realize its poignancy—an intangible, beautiful collaboration that ultimately climbs over the walls we have constructed around ourselves. Through working with others you will shed your fear of slipping away, and gain a confidence in rediscovering yourself as someone of unique value beyond the tragedy.* Okay. But jazz? *Jazz?* When they'd met by phone, Lucy had explained to Amy that her only instrument was a cello, if you could call it "her instrument," and she'd last played one in high school and only carried it with her cross-country because she liked seeing it; it suggested she could be musical when she'd make the time. But actually play it? Amy told her not to worry. For now, Lucy could double the bass line. If she could read the parts, then she'd be fine. The main requirement was a commitment to a minimum of a month's worth of rehearsals, and a final performance with a date and time to be determined.

Still waiting, Lucy goes over the score one more time. Then she glances up at the bassist. She whispers, "I guess we're the string section."

He drags his finger across the first staff, along Paul Chambers' transcribed bass line. "Note for note," he says. "Big and small."

•

69

As a little girl, she liked to watch the movie *Shenandoah* on TV. It played annually, usually on weekend afternoons, and when it did, Lucy would curl in the corner of the living room couch, a throw pillow tucked against her chest. Recently she saw it again, late one night on the classics channel when she couldn't sleep, propped against the headboard, knees drawn up to her stomach, one of the two pillows folded and bracing her neck. And even though she knew it was coming, her eyes still welled up when Boy Anderson stumbled back home from the Civil War battlefield after being believed dead.

Despite reports of its demise, Lucy is grateful for cinema. She is grateful for a place where hope always outpaces the odds.

It's been almost a full year since the attack. Some anniversary. And although somewhere in a warehouse there is rubble from the wreckage, and over that rubble stand pathologists and forensic investigators and ATF and FBI and Justice, and other experts sifting for bone fragments and traces of explosives and all other relevant matter, she has accepted that Henry never will be found. He is never coming back. And given the violent nature of the attack, she has thought over and over that this much is true: things can disappear without a trace.

In real life there are no Boy Andersons.

Still, it seems impossible to imagine, as she still lives with Henry even though he isn't there. Lucy still closes the bathroom door when she sits to pee.

•

After exactly fifty minutes, Amy stands up and like a

traffic cop throws out both palms. The drummer is the first to stop, next the woman named Phyllis on the upright piano, then the string section, with the two horns and the flute slowly trailing off, somehow reminding Lucy of a breeze dying along a long boulevard.

They'd been in a groove when Amy called stop. Who knows if it sounded any good, but Lucy would have to admit that she felt something—bowing the notes in perfect synchronization with the bassist's plucking, creating a sensation that sounded both gliding and deliberate, the way a large bird's wings will pulse while in flight.

In spite of her suspicion of this whole thing being hokum, and her instinct of Amy being a little bit of a weirdo, there is no question that when her cello and the bass fused into the rhythm, finding the beat against the steady kick drum and hi-hat, and the piano joined them on the rests, bringing about a certain hesitancy, followed by the horns floating in with the melody as moody and as brooding as a morning fog, that she'd been transported out of herself. Somewhere, maybe, for the first time in a while, outside of this world.

Amy announces, "That's our time for tonight. And you're all getting there! You nearly have the introduction down pat."

Lucy pushes up at her sleeves. The air from the fan refreshes when it blows past, so slow but then suddenly fleeting. When she next meets with her therapist, she will admit that it felt good to work over and over on something, trying to get it just right, and not have it be something that congested her mind with a million-and-one tangled and competing thoughts about who she is,

71

who she's been, and who she might be.

As the musicians put away their instruments, Amy reminds them to keep practicing over the next two days, and to journal their feelings about the experience. Amy sits back down in her chair, legs crossed, the toe of her sneaker bouncing up and down. They'll try to nail down this intro on Friday, and then next work on opening it up into the choruses where the improvising can take place. "Maybe just try listening to the original recording over and over. Try to internalize it." She then tells Lucy and the bassist they did a good job. Already they fit right in.

No one seems to be listening, more focused on packing and leaving. It is nearly eight o'clock on a Monday night. Like Lucy, most probably came straight from work, without dinner or pause.

Amy coughs to break the silence. Then she scratches at her ankle until there is a visible red streak. Lucy tries not to notice. There is something extra pathetic about being judgmental at a survivor's group in a church basement.

•

Under the glow of yellow street lamps and the backlit storefronts, it is as though Lucy has emerged from the COG stairwell into a different world from that which she'd just left. Like a children's story about entering new lands through a secret closet door. And, god, it smells funny here. But a little bit refreshing in its difference. Although this is her town, at least the town that has become her home, only now does she see how different her bohemian midtown neighborhood looks from this area, with its long flat roads, and patches of former farmlands with *for sale* billboards posted all around them, and little strip mall plazas composed of bars and minimarts and pizza places that seem on the verge of closing.

It is just her and the bassist out front on the sidewalk. He's leaned forward, a cupped hand protecting a match flame from the breeze, trying to light a cigarette. He'd asked her if she wanted one. She'd shook her head, but said she'd keep him company.

The butt finally catches, and for a split-second he disappears under a cloud of smoke, indistinguishable from his giant bass beside him. He says, "I remember you from the news."

Lucy nods. Tries to breathe evenly, and not react. It would be stupid of her to think she'd have total anonymity. Especially among a group of survivors, the world of people who actually take advantage of and dial the hotline numbers. Yet she can't keep from turning flushed. It's the same feeling as being caught in a lie. "You play well," she says, brushing the back of her hand across her forehead. "Really, really well."

"I thought I'd give it a try."

He is tall. He is slim. Remarkably youthful despite the wear on his face, or the thinning of his graying hair. Kind of like a teenager in bad light, but one who is old enough to be her father. She tells him she was a bit reluctant, but now she's kind of glad that she came. It seems like a good bunch of people, if not a mixed bunch.

He says, "One sure thing about a therapy jazz group—you can bet everyone has a story."

It takes everything she has not to ask his story. But she's uncertain of the rules. Nothing ever was articulated outside of the meeting time, the commitment to a public concert, and possessing the sheet music.

Occasional cars pass by on the boulevard. Through the thickening fog their headlights beam like perfectly rounded pipes.

He says, "It's just the textures that make it feel like something more. But at its heart, it is just a standard twelve bar blues. It's easier if you think about it that way. Simple and direct."

Lucy shakes her head. Shrugs.

"*Blue Train*. What we were playing tonight."

"It's been a long day."

He drags off the cigarette, and although it's still only half burnt down, he drops it to the sidewalk and rubs it out with his heel. "You look different and the same," he says. "From what I've seen on the news."

Lucy grabs on to the top of her cello case. Suddenly, she feels a little off balance. And just then, the door to the COG opens up, and it is the drummer carrying out his cymbals in perfectly shaped black bags with the manufacturer's logo. He's let out the stale air of the COG's basement, and it's mixing with the weird smell of the neighborhood, and she hopes for a big gust that will blow it out. Clear it out.

The drummer just says *later*, and keeps on walking. Lucy watches him go down the block and then disappear when he rounds the corner. It is quiet enough that she hears his door shut and his engine start up. She keeps her eyes down, now focusing on the crushed butt near the bassist's shoes, still smoldering. "It's a complicated time," she says.

"I didn't mean to . . ."

She straightens up. Runs a hand through the side of her hair, fingers combing, and it feels flat and listless. "None taken," she says, baffled by her choice of words.

"I guess it has been a long day." He shimmies the bass toward him, and steps forward toward the curb. "Thanks for standing out here and kind of sharing a smoke."

It now feels so lopsided, in that he knows her story, knows it well enough to be able to comment on shifts and changes, and yet she knows nothing about him. She doesn't even know his name. He says he's parked right here, pointing to a van that reads *Duncan Distributors* on the side. He adds it's his only vehicle that he can get his bass into, which makes him smile, showing a row of straight teeth that are slightly charcoaled, and translucent at the edges. As he starts toward the van, for the first time she notices his gait, a slight hobble, but one that is worn and historic. He pulls open the side door, and the logo disappears. As he slides his bass into the well, Lucy says, "Wait."

He turns around.

She takes in a breath. To hell with the rules and the protocol. "What's *your* story?" Lucy asks. She leans backward, all her weight falling to her heels.

He slides shut the door; it sounds like an old garage door slamming, all loose and crushing mechanics. "Wednesday?" he suggests. "After our next playing session?" He makes a point of twisting his wrist to look at his watch. "How about coffee on Wednesday? After the playing session."

Playing session, she thinks. Is that what we call it?

"**It is only** a possibility," the forensic archeologist explains.

Lucy phoned him back, after getting dressed but before leaving for work. She'd gotten the message when she'd come in last night; it was after jazz, and even though he said to call up to eleven, she'd been exhausted. Plus, she was wary about being drawn into another round of hope.

Now, sitting on the edge of the bed, the corner of the mattress bending down, she crosses her legs and settles in. On her tights, she notices a piece of lint, a tiny relief along the seam. Sunlight angles through the curtain. It cuts a narrow path along the floor. She wants to keep suspicious. Not fall right into the trap of expectation.

Since Edith Franks no longer works at the Archives, for once Lucy doesn't feel rushed.

It is only a possibility, the forensic archeologist repeats, but there might be something; deep within the sifted rubble, fine dust and dirt under a handheld screen, meticulously combed into vacuum-sealed plastic pouches, bag-by-bag, acre-by-acre, yard-by-yard, foot-by-foot, inch-by-inch. There may be something. "It's just a fragment," cautions the forensic archeologist. A shard, a sliver, a chip, but based on the scene documentation and mapping, there is cause for further testing, and as a courtesy he's letting her know before proceeding.

She asks, "How much *cause*?"

They've been here before. He reminds her of all

the factors that she's learned over the past year: how at the epicenters of an explosion or fire, bones become discolored, brittle, and highly fragmented, and how DNA extracted from burnt bone fragments may be highly degraded, making *an amplification of genetic markers difficult or even impossible*. They also are very prone to contamination with external DNA, meaning there lies the possibility that it never can be properly identified. In this case, the hopeful news is that the bone fragment was not fully charred, or as they say *black-burnt*, which typically leaves the DNA too degraded to be scientifically useful. The sliver they are working from is what they'd say is a *blue-gray burnt* bone, and while not typically as conclusive as, say, a semi-burnt or fully preserved bone, it does increase the odds of making an identification with an authentic profile.

When she asks about the physiological origin of the chip itself, she can tell the question makes the forensic anthropologist uncomfortable, and that it's something he'd like to avoid; he doesn't want to conflate his science with her sentient life, and so he elects to answer clinically, explaining that DNA can be extracted from the center of a tooth or from bone marrow.

They mutually understand that that is as far as the answer will get. Even when she tries to keep it straight— *black-burnt*, *blue-gray burnt*, *burnt-burnt*—he again answers with a factual generality, saying that crematorium guidelines are set for ninety minutes at a constant 1800 degrees Fahrenheit to cremate a body, and that based on the documenting and assessing of the mapped area that he is working with, that that time parameter would not have been exceeded—giving his team a glimmer of hope that they might see a positive result—but again, and he stresses *again* again, it is only a possibility.

Lucy knows the forensic archeologist is on her side. Lucy knows that he is rooting for a resolution, and that one of the draws to the sciences must be his belief that there are absolute conclusions to be drawn. But also not to be forgotten is the reality that more often than not there are impediments to ever reaching those conclusions, be they environmental, technological, or intellectual; and while the occasional conclusions are victorious, celebratory, and satisfactory, in fact it is the mysteries that propel him—the process of solving the puzzle. Lucy understands that. She wouldn't ask him to say or imply anything otherwise, nothing that would push him into the realm of being disingenuous. Still, there is one thing she wants to know: a simple, objective, empirical question: "How long will it take?"

His voice perks up. It sounds louder on the line. He says they are in the middle of an exciting time for forensic science, and that technology has greatly reduced the time the process takes, particularly in the initial steps—the milling and extracting of the DNA, because they have to get it out to be able to test it. His lab has been lucky enough to have purchased several Freezer Mills, specifically the 6750, the same one they still use in the search to ID the 9/11 missing (*still searching?*). The machine, basically, is a lab about the size of a bread machine, and what it does is cool samples to cryogenic temperatures, keeping them immersed in liquid nitrogen while it grinds and pulverizes, ensuring that the DNA itself is preserved, as opposed to the heat that might be generated through the traditional grinding process—particularly for a sample such as the one we're working with, one we might otherwise have classified as likely ungrindable, and one that in our best efforts to make it work, probably would have rendered and altered the composition of the sample as unusable. He stops. Catches himself, and says, "I don't think I've answered your question now, have I?" and proceeds to explain that the old process, the traditional grinding process, sometimes took up to twenty-four hours, but with the 6750 it's more like two or three, which means they can get the extracted sample off to the lab that much quicker, and then of course they will need to analyze, compare and match it if possible. If they are having a good week, and if they have a boss who can expedite it as a priority, he says it could be within five or six working days, but he'd give it at least ten as a minimum, because he can only attest to what happens on his end during this first stage with the grinding and extracting.

Lucy hasn't said anything. She's not sure she's taken a breath since he started talking. She picks at the lint on her stocking. It keeps moving without ever coming off.

He coughs. "Did I lose you?"

"Let's go back," she says. "Did you say grind and extract? Are you saying you need to destroy the sliver, the fragment, the chip, the shard, the whatever, in order to test it?" She stops picking when she realizes it is not lint, but a thread, one that easily could come undone. "And what if there's nothing to be seen or it doesn't belong to Henry?"

He tells her he understands her concern. "If that is the case," he says, "then they will at least have eliminated one possibility in their search for what they still don't know."

"But if it is him, if the DNA confirms it, then that means we will have had to eliminate all traces of him in order to find him." As she says that she thinks of the Victorian safety coffins that became all the rage with the cholera epidemic, equipped with bells inside for the mistakenly dead to ring should they find themselves waking up six feet underground. *Dead ringer. Saved by the bell.* And she thinks about how the prosecutors will take this, if in fact it pans out: whether they'll frame it as being a whole new loss, as though the atrocity again had just been committed; or if they'll see it as losing their most sympathetic victim, no longer the only surviving spouse of a victim who simply vanished off the face of the earth. She can only imagine how Henry's parents, anxious for this to come to end, would be forced to face an ending that instead would seem like a new beginning. She says she's not sure this is a good idea.

The forensic archeologist says he understands her concern, but as part of the long-term investigative team this is part of their mandate.

She is about to protest until she remembers that he is a scientist and this is science and while there may be questions of ethics and morality that factor in to scientific inquiry, there is no room for emotion, and right now that is all she has to back up her reasoning and reacting—emotion. She says, "Well, you did say it is only a possibility."

"Yes," he answers. "Our best lead yet. But only a possibility, indeed."

SARINA WANTS TO take Lucy out to dinner tomorrow night. "Just the three of us," she says. "You, me, and Edith's memory." They're in the first floor foyer, which serves as the entrance for the California Museum of History, around the corner from the information desk, in the alcove near the elevator. It's where they always meet to talk, holding file folders half open against their hips as their cover. Over their shoulders, covering the main floor's back wall are violet-hued plaques of inductees into the California Hall of Fame. Sometimes when Lucy looks back she sees Bruce Lee. Other times she makes eye contact with Buck Owens, David Hockney, or astronaut Ellen Ochoa.

Since the day of the attacks, Sarina has shifted into becoming Lucy's sole friend. She was there when the shootings were announced, and she had made sure to remain there in the aftermath when it seemed as though the novelty had run out for others. For that alone, Lucy is grateful, willing to overlook the surface traits of Sarina, the ones that used to grate at her. But she hasn't been able to bring herself to say anything about the forensics call. It's as though saying something is the same as conjuring something.

Sarina continues, "It will be our own going away party for Edith. *Surprise!*"

"That's not nice."

"Why, she's earned every bit of her firing."

"You mean retirement."

"*Surprise!*"

Edith Franks had taken a gamble. Doubled down on her obsession with Lucy. Ever since the morning of the shooting, when Lucy didn't come in for another two weeks, followed by a full year of sporadic days off that either were related to the investigation or to her inability to cope, Edith Franks was determined to make sure that policies and procedures trumped the individual. Otherwise, there was no system. The obsession combined her own sense of justice with the need for retribution; a response to the manner in which she believed Lucy abused her job responsibilities. Not so privately, Edith Franks had been telling people she was at her wit's end.

Lucy says she can't. Not that she can't celebrate Edith's memory. But just not tomorrow night.

"Your jazz thing?"

"Monday, Wednesdays, and Fridays."

"It's hard to picture."

Lucy is about to agree. In general, she tends to agree as a social convention. But then the problem is that she'll start to believe what she's agreed with, even if she didn't quite actually feel as such. She is just malleable enough that someone else's perspective can become a part of her. The fact is that she liked the first night of the jazz band. And in a way, it did feel a bit therapeutic. So she has to resist the temptation to just agree that going to jazz therapy is a weird thing. Instead, she says, "The bass player was nice. He was new, too."

"You didn't tell me there was a bass player."

"It's a band, Sarina."

The elevator doors open, and they both go quiet and reflexively open their file folders. You never know.

It's the guy with the big mustache from the admin side who'd sent the all-staff email announcement about Edith Franks. They didn't know his name before. Once when Sarina needed to reference him, she just curled down her index finger into a hook, and pressed it to her lip, saying, ". . . just got promoted." But he walks by without noticing them, providing some relief but also leaving a kind of a disappointment by confirming their invisibility.

They both shut their folders. Sarina says, "Tell me about the bassist."

"There are codes," Lucy whispers. "Protocol about anonymity."

"Oh, come on."

"Okay. I don't really know anything to say. He was kind was all. An older guy."

Sarina's face turns. She presses her index finger mustache against her philtrum, and whispers, "Three o'clock . . . Three o'clock! Open your files. Quick."

With folders open, the two of them put on serious faces that feign intense conversation, and it feels so overdone they both nearly burst out laughing. Sarina says, "Is this the stupidest we can be?"

Lucy nods in affirmation, the two of them a pair of sidekicks without a leader. "I'd better get back," she says.

Edith Franks probably shouldn't have gone around saying it was the "nuclear option," a term she'd heard a politician use on the news—one she clearly hadn't heard before, but since had become her catch phrase and defense, spoken always with a tinge of regret, as though she'd had no other choice. Others, like Sarina, saw it as badgering. Edith's constant reading of the employee handbook. Edith's write-ups. Edith's emails to her bosses, cc'ing Lucy, all with the subject line that read *Insubordination*. This was straight up harassment.

Sarina says, "Maybe *after* jazz tomorrow?"

Lucy cocks her head. Sarina really does see them as a duo, doesn't she? Characters searching for a new plotline.

"Our memorial," Sarina adds. "Our farewell night for Edith."

"I'm pretty sure the bass player and I are having coffee."

"Celebration postponed."

Lucy says she doesn't know about celebrating. She never wanted to make trouble for Edith. She tells Sarina she never meant to ruin someone's life.

Sarina is kind enough not to point out the irony.

•

The television plays in the background. Lucy barely listens, keeping the volume low. A PBS show about the childhood years of a pre-war president. She should be doing her homework, listening to *Blue Train*, as instructed by Amy, but she's only gotten as far as downloading it, and then burning it on a CD. (She hasn't been able to bring herself to journal; it seems too contrived.) It's hard to focus, wondering about the results of the bone samples and what it means and how it works, and also knowing that should the results be substantiated, the feds will be swooping in with something else they will ask her to do.

She sits cross-legged on the living floor, leaned back against the couch with the cello lying across her lap. She has just finished swabbing the length of the strings, trying to clean off years of old rosin. The bassist's instrument had looked so immaculate—the wood glowing, the face cared for and full of life. In comparison, her cello seemed shabby. Dust-covered and musty. Strings nearly black. It made her a little bit ashamed. With a blue hand towel that she's dampened with water, Lucy cleans the dust off the body with slow, concentric circles.

As she broadens her strokes, Edith Franks pops into her head. This isn't unusual, as Edith Franks has been with her nearly every night for the past year. A steady antagonist in a listing world. Different this time: Edith Franks isn't there anymore. In a way, it does make her feel a little sad, despite Sarina's correct assessment that Lucy had been nothing but a target. Maybe it was the way it spiraled so quickly. How sudden it felt. Two weeks earlier, word had leaked out that Edith tried to write Lucy's line out of the budget. Then Sarina took it upon herself to speak with a lawyer who was dating her neighbor and also happened to represent rank-and-file state civil service employees for SEIU Local 1000; he arranged for a cease-and-desist letter made out to Edith Franks, Edith's boss, and the State of California, threatening legal action should this constant workplace abuse persist. Late Friday afternoon there was a cut position announced, only it was Edith Franks'. The memo circulated by the Stache Man read that Edith Franks would "retire retroactively to the start of the fiscal year." Just like that, Edith Franks was gone. And despite Sarina's call for celebration and victory, Lucy can't shake feeling just a little bit empty over it, thinking about how, at the very least, Edith Franks has been the only person who treated her as someone untouched by a tragedy.

Lucy gives one continuous wipe along the face, and then holds the cello up in the lamplight. There still are some dust streaks that easily can be cleared. But most disappointing is how flat the veneer is—faded and lifeless, with the little black scratches and cracks winding through the reds and browns of the wood. With her rag, she gives one last swipe, and then lays the cello back in the case, having to give a light but firm push to press it into the preformed mold. She leaves the cover up, allowing any excess moisture to dry.

Lucy then gets off the floor, relocating to the couch. She scoots down to the far end on the left, where she won't have to see the cello. Even cleaned up, its battered condition only makes her feel lousy.

With the remote, she begins flipping through the channels, figuring a few times around will lull her into sleep, as though it is an early-twentieth-century spinning hypnosis wheel. Sleep still is hard to come by. The quieter it gets, the more space there is for voices to come into her head like some kind of tape-looped to-do list. All she wants, for now, are neutral thoughts.

Just as she starts to drift off, the telephone rings. It is well after nine o'clock. Well after the courtesy hour. *And here it begins*, she thinks, assuming word already has come in from the forensics lab. But she keeps her eyes shut, ignoring the vibrating phone on the coffee table. One more night is all she asks for. Because once she answers and the information is given, she will have crossed a line into the next phase. And so despite the urge to pick it up, Lucy lets it ring. When it stops, she stretches out, returns the channel to PBS, the adolescent years, and then slowly she fades.

Twenty minutes later it rings again, rousting her from true sleep. Could the forensics anthropologist be that determined? Lucy straightens and stretches. Rubs a little bit of spit off the side of her mouth, and wipes her palm against her pants. Seeing the open cello case, she leans forward, and with her toe nudges the top until it falls shut.

She grabs the phone off the table. The Caller ID reads *Unknown Caller x 2*.

9:25 and 9:55.

Both times it rang through until the voicemail. At neither time was a message left.

HERE'S THE PART, the part that's a truth, and the part that no one will say: she only knew Henry for two years before they were married for another three. In other words, that leaves twenty more years of his life to account for without her; and with that equation, she barely has the right to shoulder so much of this grief, or at least get so much attention for it. But it's never been Lucy's agenda to usurp Henry's parents. That has been put upon her. First, there's the media narrative of youth (young couple, young wife, an end too soon), and next the geographical fact that it took place in California, and they live in California, and the world loves California stories, location, location, location. Finally, and equally most important, is the prosecutorial narrative that the outward devastation of her loss is the icing to the government's case—attractive newlyweds, miscarriage, dream life forever ruined by an ideological madman.

Taken all together, she has become the face of tragedy.

But it is Henry's parents who deserve the true attention. They are suffering most. And Lucy knows that, and she doesn't deny it. She always welcomes them when they call, and she even pretends that prior to the shooting and the bombing that all was harmonious, despite knowing what Henry really thought of them, particularly his mother. But why litigate that? Why even keep it lodged in the back of the mind when at this point it doesn't matter? Don't they, Henry's parents, deserve to be able to make their own fiction? To own their own fiction? Because other than photo albums and videotapes and Super 8 memories, it is all they have now.

And yes, some people think it's strange that there never has been a service. Lucy's even thought it strange at times. But with so much unknown and still being investigated, and without a confirmed body, it's seemed premature and almost wrong to discuss or consider memorials or burials.

Victorian bells in Victorian coffins.

But with a year gone by, and now a formal anniversary approaching, last week, well before she would ever imagine DNA might have been discovered at the scene, Henry's father formally and pointedly requested that Lucy find a "grave site."

On the phone, she'd agreed even if she just wasn't sure what that meant.

Henry's father suggested that the plot be in California near her and Henry's home because that was where Henry blossomed as an adult, and that was the last place he called home before vanishing. Although he didn't say it, and although it didn't really make logical sense, Henry's father believed that should Henry suddenly appear, walk out of the smoke and rubble, dusty-faced and bruised and maybe even a little confused (think: Boy Anderson), he'd be more likely to find his way back if his final resting place were just a little closer walk to the last place where he lived.

Lucy just murmured in assent; she didn't try to discuss or negotiate or understand or parse his logic.

Henry's father then began pushing her to buy the adjoining plot for herself, not even considering that she is barely twenty-four, and who knows where her life will take her. Even as he spoke, a thought crossed her mind that literally wrenched her gut to the point that she had to break for the toilet and call him right back: *Who was to say that one day, nearing the end of her own life, she wouldn't have a husband of several decades and children and grandchildren, and wouldn't want to be consigned to being buried in a plot beside the man she loved and lost some sixty or seventy years back in what had seemed like another lifetime ago?*

Yes, she understands that like the prosecutors, but for different motives, Henry's parents need her to be forever tied to this story. That is part of *the* story and thus part of *their* story. And yes, she feels the pull to fulfill that function. Yet she also knows that eventually the time will come for her to break free from it, that it can't forever be her story, no matter how much it suits everyone else to keep her cast in that role.

Still, from across the country, Henry's father directed her, with his mother never taking the phone, only calling out corrections and catching her husband's every verbal mistake or misstatement. Although Lucy shared the chill Henry had about his mother, she also was aware that Henry's mother saw right through this charade, that she saw Lucy as a fraud for being the one to absorb and publicly appropriate all the grief, and when the smoke and ash finally cleared, it should only be the three of them left and reunited—Henry's father, Henry's mother, and Henry. The rest is just a blip.

From the couch, the mother's chastising was as much about deflecting her own questions of worth as it was a seething anger at watching her husband cede all the responsibility of grief to her daughter-in-law (is she still a daughter-in-law?) as a stand-in for managing his own. It didn't faze him; he just rattled off instructions. And Lucy wrote them down. He talked of a memorial. He said he'd leave the guest list to her. He spoke of music. Beatles. Stones. James Taylor. Joni. And Henry's mother bellowed out, *Those are* your *musics, for god's sake*, but he just ignored her and kept on with details that likely would be forgotten.

Lucy barely was listening. She was stuck at *guest list*. Who would she invite? Who already wasn't exhausted by this sadness? Who wasn't trying to move along? Who on Earth would want to revisit this a year later?

Henry's father saw this as the ultimate celebration. As though it would be the kind of memorial that would be televised. Lucy came to when he asked if she got all that, and she said, yes, yes, yes. He told her once she purchased a plot (life insurance covers Henry's, at least, right?), then they'd settle on a date, back into it from there, and that the two of them would come out and help with the final preparations. "That would be great," Lucy said. "Just great."

LESS THAN TWENTY-FOUR hours later, after hearing from the forensic investigator, the follow up call she was anticipating from the federal prosecutor's office comes in at her work. She asks if she can phone back at lunch, and Ray, the Assistant U.S. Attorney with whom Lucy usually speaks, says he can do one better, that he and his boss are in town for a meeting at the California Attorney General's office, and he hopes Lucy can meet them there during her lunch hour. They want to talk about the case. About pending developments and possible directions. He doesn't say anything about bone chips or DNA. Everyone from his office always talks as though they are being deposed. As though everything said might be discoverable.

She asks, "Have you talked with Henry's parents?"

"Too many cooks and all," he says. "It's best to have a single line of communication."

She really doesn't want to go. She understands their sophistication. How easily they can talk her into anything that serves their agenda, and her lack of ability to deflect them. She suggests, "Maybe there's a better cook for this kitchen."

Ray laughs in a way that seems a little too light for the situation. He says he doesn't think so. She has to remind herself that to him this is only a job.

Sarina walks by Lucy's desk. Catching Lucy's eye, she rubs her palm over her stomach, and then limps in a charade of a starving man crossing the desert, rolling her eyes back in her head. They can be such goofballs.

93

Lucy shakes her head. She mouths *can't*, and with her left hand points at the phone.

Playfully, Sarina wags her finger. In a whisper, she says, "You'll tell me all later," and then mimes someone playing a standup bass, the index and middle fingers of her right hand plucking the invisible strings.

Lucy shakes her head, and then nods yes about *later*.

During the "later," maybe Lucy finally will tell her about this possible bone chip breakthrough that she's known about for the past day, and she'll apologize for keeping it to herself but it was a lot to process, and, like a pregnancy, you don't blab the news until a number of months go by, which in this case is days—five to ten of them, according to the forensic anthropologist. And Sarina will understand because in general she does understand, but what Lucy won't say, what will be impossible for her to say because she doesn't understand it herself, is why she's so reluctant to share this new information. Maybe because it's placed her on a precipice, and the results could change everything about how she understands the situation? Or maybe because it's always seemed easier to never say anything, and while omission may not be the same as lying, it can be pretty close, because the end result is keeping a part of yourself hidden when you're promoting transparent openness. She knows she did that with Henry. For every day of the past year, she has thought about that, about how she trusted that, with time, she eventually would give herself fully to him, and then she couldn't.

As Sarina walks out, Lucy watches her from behind, so full of life, so always attentive and protective of others, and yet there is an implicit loneliness about her;

it's easy to picture her in her apartment at night when her world has gone down for the evening, so afraid and so lonely. The thought breaks Lucy's heart. Oh, Sarina, she thinks, I'm not nearly the friend you think I am.

Ray asks if she's still there.

"I'm sorry," she says. "I'm so sorry."

•

Forty-five minutes later finds her sitting in a conference room at the AG's office, following a ten-block walk down 10th to I Street, that, in the crowds and heat, felt like it took forever. She sits braced.

There are sandwiches on the table, laid out on a round plastic serving tray, delivered by a deli off J Street. Roast beef, turkey, and tomato and mozzarella. All quartered. Beside them are bags of potato chips, all plain. There is just the four of them: Lucy, Ray, U.S. Attorney Margaret Kelly, who is heading the prosecution herself, and the state's Attorney General, Whit Hopkins.

A woman the age of Lucy's mother floats in and out, checking drinks, confirming that there is enough food—all with the demeanor of a college intern intent on pleasing, laughing in a coquettish way that initially unnerves Lucy until she gets used to it.

They sit at the end of the boardroom table. The AG is at the head, the two prosecutors on the side, and Lucy, alone, facing them. When the secretary checks in, she always stands beside Lucy. For that, Lucy is grateful.

Ms. Kelly begins by thanking AG Hopkins for lending his office, following their earlier meeting. She says she thought it was best not to meet in public.

"Everything," Ms. Kelley says, "takes on meaning." It is hard not to look at her hair, a reddish brown that almost looks like a ruby, and not just in color—her hair actually is sculpted a little like the shape of a gemstone.

Attorney General Hopkins nods in agreement. Ms. Kelly adds that it was her suggestion that the AG sit in, given his expertise as a former prosecutor and a former U.S. Attorney from the Northern District before being elected. Still, it doesn't appear as if he plans to talk during the meeting. This all seems a bit odd to Lucy. But then she remembers that *The Bee* has been reporting that any day AG Hopkins is expected to declare that among a lackluster field he will enter the upcoming midterms as a Republican challenger hoping to unseat the current junior senator, a move his enthusiastic supporters and the party establishment have been pushing him to do, but one that he's avoided either through careful consideration or through a strategy of getting all the free press coverage by stringing out the *will he* or *won't he* question. And sources now are confirming he will. If that is the case, then it makes perfect sense why he wants to sit in on this, because attaching himself to the case, attaching himself to *her*, bolsters the argument that he not only will be tough on protecting Californians against terrorism, but that he has deep compassion for the victims; she still remembers his campaign slogan for Attorney General: *These are not statistics, they are people.*

Ms. Kelley says they are glad for the chance to talk, given the latest news from the forensic team. It was good of Lucy to be able to come on such short notice. She says, "I hope you'll appreciate that everything I am going to say today is purely based on our perspective, and I trust that you won't confuse it with insensitivity."

"I should say that I don't have a lot of time," Lucy says. "It took longer to get here than I expected."

Ms. Kelley says, "We can be quick."

"I thought it would be shorter, the walk."

"I'm a little concerned about the potential of this bone chip," Ms. Kelley says. "About what it might or might not confirm."

"They told me ten days. Perhaps as short as five."

"Nothing, including the timeframe, is to be counted on. You do understand that, don't you?"

"That doesn't really make any sense to me. What you're saying."

Ms. Kelley looks to Ray. It seems this has been choreographed. He is softer in tone. He is the one member of their team who ever calls Lucy by her first name. He reminds Lucy that as the surviving spouse of the only missing victim of the attacks, she is the centerpiece for the emotional argument to the jury for the death penalty. But this forensic development presents two major potential concerns: firstly, that confirming Henry's identity would alter that key aspect of their narrative just enough to soften the perception of the defendant—already perceived as being removed enough from the events to call into question his level of accountability. And secondly, and perhaps more tactically than strategically, they just can't have any aspect of the proceedings turn to putting the science on trial. It can create doubt. And one speck of doubt can do in a whole case.

"I don't understand what you're asking of me."

Ms. Kelly takes over again. "I think what we are

97

asking is threefold. Keep this recent development to yourself. Let us manage how the information gets out."

"One cook," Lucy says, nodding.

"One cook."

"But that was only one fold."

Ray asks, "What do you mean?"

"She said it was threefold. That was only one."

The AG reaches for a sandwich. His elbow knocks a pen that jets across the table and onto one of the empty board chairs.

Ms. Kelley says the second part is to hope Lucy will go through with any normal planning regarding the loss of Henry. The world continues to watch, and the best thing Lucy can do for the case is to proceed as usual, and not let the potential of the DNA results change that in any way. She says, "For example, we understand your husband's parents would like to have a funeral service, as it is near the one-year anniversary. Is that right?"

"Did I tell you that?"

Ray cuts in to remind Lucy how many investigators are on this case. It is a major counterterrorism investigation.

Lucy says nothing. It barely makes any sense as an answer. Yet she fully understands.

"I strongly encourage you," Ms. Kelley continues, "to go through with that planning." She raises a light smile meant to be sympathetic. "So go take care of it for his parents' sake, if nothing else. It's best for all of us. Go out there tomorrow. Get it in motion for them."

Lucy says she'd been planning to do that this week anyway. Tomorrow, in fact. That it hadn't occurred to her not to do it. She'd already told his parents that she would.

Attorney General Hopkins says, "Then all in all, this was nothing more than a nice excuse for us all to have lunch in my office. But if I may add my two cents: I want you to know that you are in the hands of good people here. You listen to these two beside me. They understand what's at stake. And do know that you have an ally in me, as well. Tooth and nail, I will fight for you. That's my promise to you. Together, we will show the world that the United States of America does not let Radical Islamic Terrorism define our way of life. That's my promise."

Lucy mouths *thank you*, unsure of how to respond. It seems like maybe he just declared his candidacy. She twists, but the chair doesn't turn. To Ms. Kelley, she says, "There's still a third fold."

Ms. Kelley's mouth draws up at the corners. Somehow it completely alters the structure of her face, widening it, almost distorting it. As though the bones of her jaw and her cheeks are soft tissue, malleable and able to change shape. "Third," she says slowly and deliberately, almost pouncing on the *d* at the end. "Just put all of this out of your mind. Really, just try to live your life normally. When this case starts to ramp up, and the legal system take over, there will be a point when you're called to testify, and the nature of everything will mean you'll be more in the public eye. And when that time comes it will be best if you are just yourself, without all of these unknown and unconfirmed possibilities swirling and building in your head."

"Is that a fourth fold?"

"No," says U.S. Attorney Margaret Kelly of the ninth circuit, the U.S. Attorney's Office for the District of Southern California. "Only a sub-point of the third."

When she leaves the building, heading across the Capitol Park lawn, Lucy asks herself if she held tight, if she withstood their pressure. She thinks she did okay. After all, she was planning to look into a cemetery site anyway. But then again, had she really been planning that it would be tomorrow? She replays the conversation, unable to shake the feeling of having been pushed and led at once. But upon reflection, other than asking her not to change her plans, there were no coercions or persuasions. So, why, she asks herself, does she feel as though she's just been played?

•

At the office, Sarina pops by to ask if they can have lunch tomorrow. One hand clutches the doorjamb, while she kicks her back leg up, and makes a kissing sound.

All Lucy can think about regarding her lunchtime tomorrow is finding a burial site. The idea, she now understands, has been deeply planted in her head. She makes her thumb and forefinger into a gun, and points it at her temple. "Pow," she whispers.

"Oh, come on," Sarina says. "We can start our ceremonies with the beginning of a month-long canonization: Saint Edith, Our Lady of Afflict-Us."

Lucy's lips turn dry. She can picture them cracking, like a time-lapse film of a desert floor under a high, hot sun. It burns at her that now she can't say anything to Sarina about the bone chip. Or about her meeting. It burns at her to have to be alone with all of this. It burns and burns and burns at her, as though she's been programmed to fill with a level of anxiety that will expand and expand and expand until she alone gets it settled. "Rain check?"

HERE'S WHAT THE guy at the cemetery says, he says there are some nice spots under the trees, giant oaks that give the grounds a park-like atmosphere. He says that while they may feel a little remote, they are often preferred for their sense of serenity and for their shade. He glances up from his map of the cemetery, a hand drawn schematic that marks all the possible spots, with the available ones highlighted by a dash from a green marker.

There they are sitting in a golf cart, determining which route they'll take. Both ignore the steady stream of traffic on the boulevard abutting the graveyard, a once previously quiet street that now has the roar of a small highway. Both ignore the bright red Target sign on the other side of the road and the cars creeping out of its parking lot, trying to turn left against oncoming traffic.

He is called John. He is about her age, wearing dirt-stained jeans with a big brown belt, a denim shirt, and black work boots with worn tips. Just as it should be. His hair is sandy brown, and although he probably shaved this morning, by midday he already has whiskery stubble on his cheeks. John is a groundskeeper and probably a gravedigger. He is kind. Speaks softly and confidently, but his words come carefully.

When his finger points to various areas on the map, the muscles in his forearm break through. He tells her he is authorized to show the available plots, explain the process, and even begin the paperwork and take a deposit, but full payment and full contracts will have to be with Gary, and best by appointment, as Gary manages two other cemeteries and a drop-in visit is not one to be counted on.

Lucy studies the map, seeing it as an odd little handmade village that resembles the orientation to the Hundred Acre Wood at the beginning of *Winnie the Pooh*. Without connecting or relating it to the very spot of land where they sit, Lucy points at a demarcated tree on the paper. She's drawn to it for the way that it is part of the grave community, while being slightly set away from the congestion. She leaves her finger on the space, as though staking a claim. "John," she says. "I think I'm interested in this one."

He glances down at the map, and then up and to the left (is it south?) before again looking down and studying the legend on the page. "It's a pretty spot," John affirms. "And there are some vacancies there."

"Can we look at it?"

"You should know it's not an easy locale," he explains. "Mostly on account of the root system of the tree. I don't think that perimeter ever was intended to be part of the main burial ground. It's just naturally expanded with need."

"I guess we'll see."

"We certainly can look. But whether it's available will depend on your needs."

"My needs?"

"For example, if you are looking for a companion plot, due to the roots we'd probably have to look at going two deep. Simply put, one on top of the other. Just not enough space for side by side. But if you are considering cremation, the options expand considerably, as there is much more ready real estate to work with for a standard urn. Only of course if we're considering that particular location. On that note, if you are thinking about cremation I should add that there also is the mausoleum."

"Too bureaucratic."

"Well, let's just go take a look. You'll let me know which options seem best for you."

Lucy nods along. She has no idea how to respond. She only knew how to be the victim of terror. She's still learning how to be a widow.

John, certainly sensitive to these kinds of conversations as a professional consideration, starts up the golf cart, and he says to hold on, they will be backing up.

She hears the beep-beep-beep of driving in reverse. She grips the frame of the cart, aware that she could bounce off, despite how smooth John is taking it. How is she supposed to know the best option for her? A little breeze blows against her face. It makes her feel trapped and contained. "I don't know how to answer," she blurts out.

John veers suddenly to the right, avoiding a small sedan, American-made. It has barreled up the driveway, and now is stuck, trying to find a way to turn around. It's impossible to see the driver. Between a combination of sun and shadows, its windows have turned to mirrors.

He stops the cart and waves to the driver, pointing out an inlet in the driveway, a little farther up past the office building.

Looking back, he tells Lucy it happens all the time.

"People rush out of the Target lot and turn into our drive because they can't get into their lane in time, thinking this might be a cut-through over to Broadway." He lets the sedan back up, then go forward toward the inlet. A car that size will take several maneuvers.

He starts up on the cart, swinging wide away from the sedan. John knows his presence only makes the driver that much more frazzled.

The golf cart drives briefly along the edge of the grass, and then back to the macadam. It goes from smooth to rumbling. "This," he calls back to Lucy, "can be a confusing time for many people."

"The reason I don't know how to answer is because there isn't an answer." She feels her voice start to disembody, hearing it as though someone else is speaking. "We don't even have any remains. None have been found." She figures that is okay to say. The U.S. Attorney's Office wouldn't mind. It is part of the planning.

The cart slows down, bumping up over a curb, and then climbing back onto the lawn. To the right is the main cemetery, rows of gray headstones and markers decorated by planters of pink and yellow plastic flowers. "If you don't mind my asking . . ."

"It's been one year."

"And I'm sure you're aware . . ."

"I know the law says seven years. But due to the unique circumstances, there has been a dispensation given by the federal government. We have a death certificate."

"I had to ask."

"I don't blame you."

They pull up under the tree. The canopy is thick and watchful. You could almost forget the road nearby, and the waylaid Target drivers pulling in and out of the driveway. John helps Lucy out. She has the urge to hug him. Hug him for the compassion he shows for someone else's tragedy even though he's likely never known his own. Hug him for the tragedies that eventually will touch him, and in which all of his professional experiences he'd been counting on to get him through will only let him down. But instead, she steps on a thick root that perfectly fits the arch of her foot.

John explains while a burial without remains is not a common practice, it also is not unprecedented. Typically, he says, it is handled in one of a few different ways. Some surviving family members have chosen to bury an empty casket. Others might bury an urn with something meaningful inside. And others simply choose to place a marker on the spot. "There is no right. There is no wrong."

Lucy walks a half circle around the tree. The ground is uneven. The grass vague and thin. This little section is less pristine than the more manicured area of the central location. A little more of an outlier, and something about that makes her think it would be perfect for Henry—or at least for the situation, given how everything about her life in the aftermath of the shooting and bombing has existed in the outskirts, slightly shaded and not quite in view. She kneels down and pats a bare patch of ground, with just a few grass blades managing through. She strokes them, and they bend backward, and then spring back to life when she withdraws her hand.

A horn blares from across the lawn. It's the same car, the American sedan, still in the driveway, now backing out toward the street after giving up on trying to turn around. How can it accelerate backward so recklessly and blindly into the traffic with such earnest conviction and authority?

"Did you say we could put an urn anywhere here?" Lucy asks. She draws an X in the bare patch. "Like maybe right here?"

SHE RAN LATE while driving to the COG. Ran late while looking for parking. Ran late while trying to drag her cello out of the back seat. Ran late to the COG basement while trying to hustle up the sidewalk, and tread down the stairwell, cello case banging between the railing and her leg. Ran late while setting up and tuning and jumping into *Blue Train*.

All afternoon she'd run late. Between the paperwork and the uncertainty at the cemetery, her lunch hour had extended well beyond one o'clock. On the way back to the Archives, she'd had to stop by her house to pick up her cello, thus making her even later. Talk about the house that Jack built. And it was only Wednesday.

Her entire afternoon had been nothing but a saga-length back-and-forth exchange with a historian in Maryland looking for specific transcripts and trial exhibits from the Robert Kennedy assassination investigation report, finally culminating in taking his order, making photocopies, and having to phone him back three times when his credit card came back rejected (a matter of two inverted numbers, which seemed sloppy for a researcher, but for some reason left her feeling a little empty). Once the manila envelope was sealed and in the outbound mail envelope, she dashed down to her car, and into the evening traffic to the COG.

Didn't even check her home email. Or her phone.

•

"I think we sounded pretty good tonight," the bassist says from across the table in a diner booth just blocks from the COG. Seated against the window, they can see his van parked out front, where the instruments are stored safely. It is windy outside, but you would only know by the leaves shimmying on the branches. Otherwise, it looks still. In the dark, the boulevard looks like a river. The sidewalks like its shores.

Finally, she's learned the bassist's name is Edgar. Her tardiness to both playing sessions had preempted introductions. It had been awkward, as he seemed to know her name. She only picked his up tonight through a comment Amy made, not via any proper introduction.

Edgar's elbows lean on the edge of the gray Formica, its top patterned with little interlocking boomerangs. Both coffee cups sit on spongy paper coasters. He continues, "Yes, pretty good for a bunch of head cases."

"Excepting the drummer."

"Yes, excepting the drummer."

Lucy adds, "It was relaxing." Immediately, she wishes she hadn't said that. It sounded stupid; something to fill the air. Think before you talk.

Edgar says he thought they really got going when they went into the improv section. He thinks it's the same amount of choruses, eight, that Coltrane played, including the tempo change midway at the fourth, double-timing. He says, "It transports you. Makes you forget what you want to forget, and remember what you don't want to forget."

Lucy sips at her coffee, but it's cooled too fast, making it taste dirty. Sometimes she wonders if she is the object of others' pareidolia—instead of her seeing faces in clouds or hearing messages in random sounds, people she's engaged with view her with *their* own perceived images, and hear from her what they want to hear.

She reminds Edgar he was going to tell her his story. What brought him here.

"Right," he says. "We all have a story."

"And since you already seem to know mine . . ."

He puts his hands on each side of the seat, and pushes himself forward. The bench, a shiny yet worn red naugahyde, squeaks and whistles. He drums both his index fingers on the table's edge. "Is that how this works?"

"Look, if you don't want . . ."

He begins to explain, "Some people who are old enough, and from around here, may know my story. The same as they know yours." He says it was in the early nineties. A protest at the Capitol, and he'd been beaten up by a crazy man. It was all random. He hadn't intended being at a rally, and this guy started clubbing the first person he saw. "A case," he says, "of being in the wrong place at the wrong time." It took a lot of years to recover, both from the injuries to his knees and to his head. The crazy man seemed to know the most vulnerable places. "But," he says. "That's backstory. Not really why I'm here." He pauses. Glances around the room, he makes slow eye contact with the waitress, miming the pouring of coffee. He withholds the next part of his story until she ambles over, the steaming carafe in her hand. Edgar understands the principles of drama. Then he looks Lucy in the eye. "Sometimes it helps to know the backstory."

110

"Right."

"Now I'd imagine you want to know why I am here."

Lucy nods twice. The anticipation is exhilarating and terrifying. She is nowhere but in his world. And though she knows it is his life, a real life, and though she knows it's wrong to feel such a way, for the moment she is glad to be in someone else's tragedy.

He begins by telling the story of his sister, Erin. A free spirit of sorts. On a lark she up and moved to New York with some guy almost twice her age. And then she disappeared. Flat-out gone. And then with near perfect timing, almost eyeballing her as he says it, Edgar asks, "Do you remember the first World Trade Center bombing?"

Just the word *bombing* jolts her into her world. It causes her to tumble back into the maze of the funeral, the anticipation, and the way it felt like a miracle of the human body that she could function for the past year when at least once a day she would lower her cold, sweating palm against her chest, and she'd swear that her heart wasn't beating.

"For a while, despite what everyone was saying, I believed Erin disappeared in that bombing. Even though all the victims were identified, all the missing people accounted for, I believed she was missed somehow. And I knew because I saw her on the television."

Lucy reaches for her coffee, but then stops. Is he saying this on purpose? For a reaction? She can barely stand to hear any more. Stop. Stop. Stop. Stop. Stop. It's like dangling over a cliff, holding on for dear life by grasping the hand of the person who's just pushed you over.

111

"All of these people—the police, the investigators, the hospitals, even my own family—they forever told me I was mistaken. They told me she'd just cut us off. It's as though they were willing her to disappear, but not the way that I knew she had. To them, what they believed was enough. They were done with explanations. For them, it was like *isn't disappeared, disappeared?*"

She grips the water glass, fog forming between her fingers.

"That's how I ended up here. Because, and I'm pretty ashamed to admit this, I gave up. I got worn down by questioning everything and everybody. Of seeing every situation as suspicious. Of believing Erin would be in touch at any given minute, and being afraid to step out of a room because the phone might ring, or the doorbell might chime. Of realizing she wasn't rushing to be in touch. And so I quit on her. And then not only did I have to figure out how to live with that, I had to figure out how to live with other people not giving a shit that I gave up. Outside of doing my job, I don't think I talked to a living soul after I made that decision. Something needed to change. I needed to connect with the world again. It seemed like music was a good start. You don't have to talk too much. And so that's why I'm here." He lifts his mug, puts it back down again, and leans back, receding into the banquette as if he'd dropped his own curtain.

It's hard to know how much to believe, if he's really decided to give up and forget, or if he's figured out that he'll be left alone if he says as much. Maybe trying to believe it makes it that much easier to cope? Either way, Lucy realizes he was not saying any of this to get a rise out of her. It was about trust. About connection. And his forthrightness and honesty compel her. It feels like the first true and unfettered conversation she's had since the shooting and bombing.

Edgar glances up at her, as though not expecting anything other than to see she's still there, and then reaches for his coffee. He says, "And that's my story."

With almost little distinction between her thoughts and her words, Lucy blurts out the details from the phone call about the DNA. She finds she is telling it just to say it. She expects nothing from him. As she nears the end, she vaguely recalls the sickening feeling she felt the one time that she went home with a strange man, and how it wasn't the sex that had shamed her, but the fact that for some reason she'd told him everything that was important to her at the time.

Edgar just sips coffee. Listening. His face makes barely an expression, but it doesn't seem cold or numb or analgesic, instead it looks intent on not showing judgment. And she goes on to explain about her meeting with the prosecutors and the attorney general, and what their strategy is, the threefold plan, and how she's supposed to be part of it even though she's not really sure she wants to be part of it, and how she's supposed to go ahead with the funeral for an empty casket, but this little piece of news about possible DNA, the news that actually could bring about some clarity for her much more than any death penalty conviction, is the one that she is supposed to keep to herself. Not to mention the creepy feeling she got from the AG, silently observing as though taking notes, and only speaking at the end to make what sounded like an implied partnership with her in his unnamed quest for higher office.

Edgar pushes his coffee mug onto the table. The bottom knocks the metal creamer, causing a small uprising of milk to puddle on the table. Frustrated, he looks at it, and then dabs at the pool with his wadded up napkin. He's shaking his head with a velocity that increases with such acceleration that to Lucy it looks as though his skull could loosen, pop off, and launch across the diner. "No," he finally speaks. "Absolutely not." He rolls the napkin to the middle of the table. "You have to trust me on this."

She leans back as he inclines in. "I don't . . ."

"Don't let the government take him from you, too." Edgar looks serious enough to cry. "They will tell you it's about justice. That it's about right and wrong. But it's about their careers. Especially with the upcoming election. Don't take any of them at their word. Whit Hopkins is no different than Rudy Giuliani. When Rudy was U.S. Attorney and went after the mafia and those Wall Street crooks, it was all grand and good until he turned his famed *perp walks* into his own red carpet. Christie. Sessions. Spitzer. They all rode the same job to a higher office. Whit Hopkins is the same. Don't trust any of them. They're all defining you and your husband for the sole purpose of defining themselves—trotting you out to show off their own agenda—all without any actual commitment or concern for you. You know?"

Lucy can only look at him. His determination. His demeanor, like a pair of giant arms that hug you and hold you in. Like a firm whisper in the ear that wants confirmation of allegiance. And he again repeats the rhetorical *you know?* because she is supposed to know, especially after the story he just told her about his past. She can only stare at him, knowing that deep down she may not want to have this answer to the bone chip mystery, partially because never knowing is an oddly safe place to be, and partially because not knowing gives her purpose, something she has no guarantee of in any other future scenario.

Now he's nodding, and again he says *you know?*, and there's a thought that's forming in her head, and she knows its intention, she knows the words, but she can't make them come out, which is, in its own way, a kind of irony, because all she is trying to say, all she's been trying to get out is: *I* don't *know.*

•

When finally she is home, Lucy collapses on the couch. The closing plea of the coffee exhausted her. The cello stands on end by the door. Beside it, her coat blankets her shoes, having missed the hook when she came in. She hasn't turned on the lights. It is a kind of violet dark. You can see the outline of everything in the room—the table lamp and its hangdog shade, the TV pressed up against the wall, a book, two magazines and a vase with weeping stems on the coffee table. The curtains hang off the window without quite touching the floor, every pleat looks like its own shadow.

She is turned around by Edgar's defiance. His conviction. Lucy needs to believe that the feds are working on her behalf. That they are trying to bring this to an end for her. But Edgar has planted a seed of doubt. Cultivated her own suspicions about people's inherent selfish determinations, the survival-of-the-fittest molecule encoded in every strand of DNA. She wants to believe that the government prosecutors do separate their strategies from their motives. But instead she sees the possibility of every word and action being a potential ruse—one that will forever preserve her as the distraught widow, in order to maintain ownership of Henry's story for their own agenda.

She takes her phone out of her purse. Two emails from Henry's father. She's in no mood to look at them. She is half expecting to see a message from the U.S. Attorney's Office wanting to know why she spilled the beans tonight.

There is only one call, again from the *Unknown Caller*. This time, however, there is the big bright red "1" showing a voicemail. It appears to have come in at just a minute after one o'clock. She pushes the icon, and listens on the speakerphone. At first, there is a lot of wind, the sound of an engine, and then the rumbling of traffic. There comes a cough, followed by the unmistakable voice of Edith Franks, first clearing her throat, and then speaking. It is a simple message; a conjoined tone of threat and satisfaction. Edith Franks simply says, "I see you still have no respect or concern for the *hour* in lunch hour." The engine noise takes over, followed by a blaring horn, and a fumbling yet abrupt hanging up.

Lucy should be scared. She should feel threatened. Intimidated. She should get up and look out the window. Maybe even call the police. Or at least Sarina. But instead she draws the phone up to her ear, presses the icon to repeat the message, and listens to it again,

again, again, and again, thankful to have Edith Franks back in her life.

SHE IS UP early, too early, awoken by rain pinging against the windows and the creepy yellow light coming through the curtain. She decides to call Henry's father, already awake hours by this point, given the time difference. She's avoided his emails, particularly since she learned about the bone fragment; Lucy doesn't like the idea of having to withhold the information from him. The responsibility is unnerving.

On the other end, the phone fumbles, and Lucy can hear both of Henry's parents, and the mother is saying *you talk with her*. There is a brushing sound, a crumbling, wrinkling noise, and Henry's father comes on, his voice out of breath and hurried. "You're up early," he says.

She reaches forward and parts the curtain, looking at the rain falling, and the stream trailing down her driveway, under her tires, and into the gutter where it flows out with the usual runoff, picking up leaves and twigs and potato chip bags. Already she can feel herself falling back into the role of the compliant daughter-in-law, obligating and deferential and demure, but for whom any hint of defiance would be categorized as prickly or moody. She says, "It's the middle of a busy week."

He says, "I sent you emails."

"I thought it would be easier to call."

"So what did you find out?"

"There's a nice space in a nice, pleasant cemetery."

"And it's near your house?"

In the background, she hears Henry's mother

saying, "What does it matter, Ed?"

Lucy gives him the exact location, and the directions from her house. She'd looked it up on an online map, ready for him. Charted the driving time, the walking time, and the bus route. She lists them in order to Henry's father. After each one, he mutters, "That's good . . . That's good."

Lucy glances at the clock. She's still in her robe, and she'll need time to shower. Traffic will be murder with the rain. Parking even worse. She tells him she put down the deposit. She tells him about the man named Gary, and how she can only sign final papers with Gary.

"And do we know when this Gary works?"

Henry's mother asks, "Who is Gary?"

Lucy says, "I am on it."

"Well you need to be. You don't want to lose the space because this Gary keeps erratic hours."

"I will. Don't worry, please. But, Ed . . ."

"Is it money? Do you need some money for this?"

"No, Ed . . . No . . . I'm just wondering if we should wait a little longer, I mean, with the trial and everything . . ." She can't bring herself to mention the forensic possibility.

"Jesus Christ with those people. We're not going to live our life around them. If they're pressuring you, I can speak with them."

"Who can talk with who?" Henry's mother is asking. "Talk about what?"

He tells his wife it is nothing. Just some bureaucratic clutter that is procedural. For being as bombastic as he is, Lucy does appreciate there is enough sensitivity in him to read his wife's anxiety and to be able to tamp it down. In that way, he reminds her of Henry, his son. And she hates not being able to tell them about the potential identification of the bone chip. It's an omission that seems cruel.

He declares, "So let's start thinking about dates."

For the moment, she wants to live up to how Henry's father sees her. It feels like the kindest thing to do. "Let me settle all the details first, at the cemetery."

"With this Gary fellow?"

"I'll track him down. I'll try to take care of it at lunch today." She promises she'll be in touch when she has more information to share, but, in order to keep honorable to herself, she doesn't say anything further about a definitive date for the service, not with the forensic test pending. It could change everything for them. She doesn't want to look back and see that she lied or blatantly misled.

As she hangs up the phone, she still can hear them talking. *Who is Gary? She is* tracking *him down. Does she know what she's doing? I'm worried she's in over her head? Can you pick up the remote, it's behind the chair. It's too much for her. Why don't you just take over?* Lucy listens for a little bit longer until their words just become the sound of their voices, and their voices just become the rhythm of the rain, and the phone abruptly hangs up and there is the fizzing of dead air.

By the time Lucy reaches her desk at the Archives, the RFK Assassination man already has left three messages, saying in a variety of ways that he hasn't heard back from anybody on the status of his documents order, and that he hopes that the credit card hassle has not jeopardized the processing, or moved it to the back of the line, or found it completely deleted all together. He would appreciate some form of confirmation. That's all he wants, he says. Some form of confirmation.

Lucy sits halfway turned to the wall, leaned back, wedging off her right shoe, which is wet after stepping in a puddle that had been camouflaged by the train tracks in the middle of the street. It is damp mostly around the toe; the sock is dark and now thick.

Sarina pokes her head in the doorway. She says, "Here's to almost getting through the new week . . . Our first week without Edith."

Lucy swings her chair around. "Maybe Edith's unleashed this rainstorm."

"Next," Sarina says, "will come the locusts and the frogs."

"Wait. Who are the good guys here?" She's tempted to say something about Edith's message. But she knows it only will rile Sarina into calling her lawyer friend, unleashing a whole new chapter of this otherwise mundane story.

Sarina smiles. She asks about how coffee with the bass player went last night.

Lucy says, "It was coffee with the bass player on a Wednesday night."

"That's all I get?"

"It's all there is to tell."

After Sarina leaves, Lucy dials the RFK Assassination man. He says he wonders if anybody there is keeping track of things. She stretches out her foot, wiggling her toes to warm them. She explains that his documents were photocopied and mailed, and that his credit card was processed, and probably will not be posted until later today, due to it having been placed after three o'clock. He says a tracking number or order number might have helped. She starts to explain that they are not a retail outlet, and instead a government agency providing a public service, but she stops short because she hears his breathing get heavier and heavier, and as with many of the RFK document hunters, he likely is among the ilk who are seeking to prove a conspiracy, and any talk of governmental procedure not only reinforces that, in fact it enflames and enrages it. Instead, she does the bureaucratic version of playing dead; she tells him she certainly will forward his suggestion to her supervisor. He says it's not a suggestion, it's a complaint. She says, in that case, sir, consider your complaint noted.

•

Gary isn't there. Gary was supposed to be there. Gary usually is there on Thursdays. There must have been a lot of activity over the past two days. It must have been all that activity that drew him to the other two cemeteries that he manages, because he has been at both of them this morning, bouncing back and forth between Florin Road and Sunrise, Sunrise and Florin Road. But he's supposed to be there, and he certainly will be after lunch; he has an appointment with a family at two o'clock.

There was an unusual amount of activity these past few days, John keeps saying, an unusual amount, as though *an unusual amount* is a middle-ground, compromising point they both can accept and agree on, given the circumstances. He asks if she can be there after

122

two. He says he'll make sure Gary stays. Make sure Gary has the paperwork ready and prepared for signatures. It won't take long once he has it in order. Gary is sensitive that way, he understands the needs of families in their times of mourning. In fact, it is that very trait of Gary's that has kept him running pillar to post all morning. So unusual, John says. This isn't how we operate.

He says he will give her his personal cell phone number. And she tells him, no that's okay. But he insists, already pulling out a business card from his wallet, bent at the corners and wrinkled down the middle. Leaning forward, resting the card on his knee, he writes the phone number on the back in big blue script that happens to slant with the direction of the wind.

He suggests she should call before leaving for the cemetery. Then he will personally walk over to Gary, and let him know when to expect her.

Lucy says she won't be back today. Her lunch hour is ending, and she'll need to be back soon. But maybe tomorrow. Probably tomorrow. There's an expectation from the parents, she explains. She needs to get it done.

John says the offer still stands. If you need to come tomorrow at lunchtime to meet with Gary, then you phone me, and we will make sure it works. If it just can't, can't, can't work, then Gary will fill out the papers as much as he can, and he will instruct me on what to do with the rest.

She tells him he is kind.

He apologizes, saying he really hates the idea of her time having been wasted.

No, she says, it's okay; it's a beautiful day. And it is a beautiful day now that the rain has cleared. The air is crisp. The sky is a delicate blue, with little wisps of clouds that look like frosting or lace. The greens pop in the grasses and the leaves, and the browns and grays of the tree barks look as though they've been hand-colored in a studio.

John offers that as long as she's here, maybe she'd like to go look at the proposed plot again.

The lunch hour is drawing down—you can tell by the way the cars start to stream out of the Target parking lot *en masse*, just as lunch bills are getting paid *en force* in restaurants all over town at this moment. She really needs to get going, but that is not why she doesn't want to go see the spot again. It would be impossible to explain. How could John understand that in her mind she's already ascribed the plot to Henry, and for just a little bit of time, just for the end of a lunch hour if it's not too much to ask, she'd rather not grieve?

Traffic was light coming back to the Archives. Nearing the parking area, Lucy sees it is seven minutes before one. She calculates that this would put her at her desk almost precisely at the end of the lunch hour. But instead, she drives past the parking space, motoring several blocks up the street, and turning right to make a gigantic loop.

She is stopped by bells and a dropping level rail as the commuter train rumbles by. Lucy waits, not bothered, watching the clock tick by, two minutes before one.

Finally, she is able to go, and she takes two more right turns, ending up back at the original parking space at exactly one o'clock.

She sits in her car, waiting for the clock to show one minute past. At almost the exact moment that it turns, her phone rings. It is Edith Franks's *Unknown Caller*. Just as Lucy hoped. For the moment, all is right with the world.

MAN, DO THEY rip through *Blue Train*. Man, are Lucy and Edgar right in sync during the introduction, not just anchoring the bottom but also guiding the whole ensemble. While they play, she pictures them as a pair of wings, and that is what they are doing, they are letting the music glide and float above the surface of the world.

It is as if her bowing is inseparable from Edgar's plucking, and it forms a kind of richness, one that almost makes her feel as if she belongs here. She knows she's not that good. She knows she only reads well enough to maintain in a high school orchestra, often stumbling and catching up a few notes behind. Yet she's transcended the mechanics of playing. Instead, it's as though she's listening, but listening from inside, as if the whole piece is being composed and played from within, and the vibrations are not from wood or strings or reeds, instead from the physiology of humanness.

In those moments, particularly as it moves into the middle improv sections, and slides into its walking bass line, she soars above the no-man's land in which her grief and suffering are okay. No longer a burden to others. No longer shamed by still being haunted by it at every single minute of every single day.

But only nearing the end does she again become aware that she is but a product of the mechanical— nothing more than a coin-operated machine from a penny arcade, lowering the bow to the strings, and pushing and pulling in prefect rhythm until the end, where she will lift her arm, lower it to her side, and let her head drop, chin into her chest.

But man, for a while did they play well.

Everything stands still. On pause. Amy leans forward, the tip of her tongue snaking in and out of the corner of her mouth, making notations, flipping pages forward then backward then forward again. Everyone is waiting.

Edgar leans over and whispers, "So, did you tell the feds to shove it? That they weren't taking this away from you too?"

Lucy says, "At this point I haven't even spoken with them."

"At this point?"

"I've been working."

"And yet another day goes by." He plucks the open E string, and it pops out and then snaps back, leaving residual sonorous vibrations that rattle the wires on the bottom of the snare drum with a nervous sizzle.

Amy glances up, peering over the top of her frames.

Edgar looks down, mouthing that he's sorry. He is oddly and quickly deferential in the face of authority. It's as though he's rubbed his eyes and a mask has come off to reveal a petulant but repentant child. Quite different than the defiant posture he presumed over coffee the other night.

Amy says they are going to take this one more time, then they'll need to move on to the second piece. We can't give a one-song performance. And speaking of, Amy adds, she's thinking the upcoming performance may be much more well-attended than she had anticipated. She expects more than friends and family.

This makes Lucy a little nervous. She's pretty sure

Amy is looking at her, silently communicating that there is extra interest because she's spread the word that Lucy is in the band. In the end, it will be good for everybody by bringing attention to this work. Lucy looks down at the spindly feet of the music stand. Trying to will away this possibility and this extra-sensory conversation. Jazz Therapy wasn't supposed to be a public deal. It was supposed to be a private healing process. How did this happen? Did she miss something in the plan that changed? She's nowhere near ready for this kind of thing.

Amy says, "I guess it goes to how good you are. Now, let's go . . ."

Everyone looks to the drummer to count off the intro. "It doesn't feel urgent to me," Lucy whispers to Edgar.

A one. And a two . . .

He bends over his bass toward Lucy, close enough that his bark can remain a whisper. "Tell me you're not falling for that crap . . . I mean, didn't you hear today's news?"

She shakes her head. "I haven't had a moment."

"Whit Hopkins officially launched his senate campaign. It's so obvious and so clear why he was there with you. You don't think every decision or plan about what they're doing with you and the case isn't being made with consideration of how it will push up Hopkins's poll numbers?"

On four, the high-hat and the horns roll in.

"I can't imagine that it's so . . ."

"Don't let them use you."

Amy calls out to hold it. "Basses! Where are you?

From the top. Again."

At the end of the rehearsal, Lucy packs her cello, half-turned from Edgar. They were supposed to go out for coffee, something she'd managed to put off until next session, after the weekend on Monday night. She was tired. She wasn't in the mood for his admonitions about how she was handling things. And, ever since she'd heard his story about his sister, she couldn't drop the idea that he was overlaying his issues on to her.

She needs a break. But she worries she's been roped and tied, and that he isn't going to let go easily.

GARY'S NOT THERE, and John the gravedigger says because it's Monday to try back at 11:30. When at 11:30 Gary still isn't there, Lucy tries John's personal cell phone, but it goes straight to voicemail. She thinks she might just go there anyway, but the thought of losing her lunch hour to the cemetery again unnerves her, and she hates how much she has been spinning and spinning and spinning her wheels waiting on other people's agendas.

Trying to take some command of her situation, she tells Barbara at the desk that she's stepping out for a moment, grabs her purse and goes downstairs where the cell reception is stronger and there is a little more privacy. She dials the forensic pathologist, looking for results, and, already deciding that if they are a positive match, that not only will she defy the U.S. Attorney's plea for discretion, but that she will walk straight to the AG's office where they'd met, stand on the very steps in an act of deliberate defiance of his having scheduled a meeting to lay claim to her tragedy, and phone Henry's parents with the news. Then she will shout it at the top of her lungs, not just for Hopkins to hear, but loud enough that it will travel south down Interstate 5, like sound vibrations through a phone wire, penetrating all the way into the offices of the Ninth Circuit, where they will know that she is alive, and for just this moment, her marriage is, as well.

The pathologist answers on the second ring. His voice sounds hesitant, not nearly as fixed and rote as

130

on the first call. It's as though he's lost the script, and is busy searching for his lines. He says there is no news yet; it is too soon. He did say it would take some time, didn't he? If he didn't, he says, he should have. She asks, Didn't you say five days, maybe? And he answers, But I'm sure I also said it could be ten, which, still, would be optimistic. He adds that he doesn't think she should be calling him directly. His words start to fumble, dropping in and out of the sentences, misplaced as he tries to gather his thoughts. After some sputtering, some false starts, he tells her that her questions are best addressed directly to the U.S. Attorney's Office, because they are the ones handling the investigation. But he has no answer for: *Why, then, did you call me in the first place?* It is clear, painfully obvious, that just as her grief over her husband is no longer personal and instead something to be managed, so is the science behind it.

The light rail comes rumbling down S Street, its warning bells dinging. It pulls up right in front of her. A boy, maybe four, maybe five, is sitting at the window directly in her line of sight. For a moment they stare at each other. The reflection of her face on the window nearly overlays his.

She hangs up on the forensic pathologist, and tucks the phone into her purse. When she looks up the train is pulling away. She doesn't see the boy in the window anymore. Just in case, she waves anyway.

Lucy turns around and starts walking. Aimless. She turns right on 10th until realizing that she's heading straight into the center of the Capitol lunch rush, and where, according to the news, later today Whit Hopkins will be making the formal announcement of his candidacy. She takes her first right on R, and just keeps walking straight, past the old warehouses that have now been converted into trendy restaurants and cafes, but on whose sidewalks, around the bases of their carefully chosen trees, one can still see hypodermic needles and spent bottles of Thunderbird.

At 13th Street she turns right again, and she is willing to keep walking in circles all day long. She marches up to X Street, extending her route, and then takes another right, walking past rows of Victorian houses chopped up into apartments.

Lucy continues walking the circle through the lunch hour, only willing to stop for Edith Franks. She will not stop for the U.S. Attorney. She will not stop for Henry's parents. She will not stop for Sarina. She will not stop for Gary at the cemetery or John the gravedigger. She will not stop for Edgar the bassist, Amy, or anything else to do with Jazz Therapy. Edith Franks is the only one with boundaries. With principles or with rules. Only Edith Franks understands having a sense of order. And so Lucy walks. Waiting for a call from Edith Franks that won't seem to come, no matter how far she gets past the lunch hour.

Maybe even Edith Franks has tired of her. By now Lucy's tragedy has fused into the tragedies of the balance of the past year. One of the many stories. People she worked with have died from cancers. Others lost parents. Spouses. And on the news, there were nightly reports of bombings and shootings and rages that took innocent lives in mass, showing endless snapshots of the victims from their weddings, birthday parties, children's graduations. (Which ones did they show of Henry? She barely can recall.) Lucy's story is no longer seen as the only story to those around her. Maybe because after the initial hassles with Edith (when she'd been going back and forth to Southern California to meet with investigators, the trip to North Carolina to see her parents, the ongoing funeral discussion, the quick responses when the forensics people called thinking they had something), she'd gone back to work, if only to busy herself and to feel normal. And there, people saw her as normal, as someone who had *managed well*, who had *sprung back*, who had a *strength to be admired because I can't even imagine if it were me. . .* Maybe it put her into the no-man's land in which her grief and suffering were almost burdensome to some . . . Maybe it even forced her to hide her agony, ashamed to show that she was still being haunted by it at every single minute of every single day, prompted by every little gesture, from the sound of a ticking wristwatch in a meeting that sounded like Henry's, to a gesture from a stranger in a lunch line, to the song of an unknown bird that she heard every morning outside her bedroom window when the news first came. Sometimes she's felt like a surging million-watt buzz of electricity, one that threatens to blow her apart and yet is invisible to all.

After her ninth trip around the downtown blocks, she heads straight to her car. Inside the Archives she has left her gray overcoat, its pockets filled with receipts that she's stuffed inside following nameless transactions that might only tell the story of an ordinary life—groceries, coffee, a packet of mints, an ATM receipt that shows amounts withdrawn and her checking account balance. They speak nothing about tragedy or grief. They don't show the trail of pressure points meeting before an oncoming emotional explosion. The Archives can keep the jacket and the receipts. Isn't it a part of the state's history?

The engine growls on start up. She reaches into her purse one last time to check the phone. Come on, Edith. You have me dead to rights.

Nothing. But she is done waiting.

Quickly she swings into the right lane, drives about twenty yards, flicks up her blinker, and makes a U-turn in the middle of the road, and heads straight to her home. She has no plan to ever return to the Archives. No plan to talk with Sarina again, but not from spite or hurt or malice, but out of kindness. Lucy is no friend to her. Sarina became a cane on which she could balance herself while she hobbled around. It only is cruelty to pretend it's anything otherwise.

Her heart is pounding. This might be the first time in how long that she has turned her back on anything.

She pulls into her driveway, crooked, the driver's-side tires parked on the edge of the brown and brittle grass. Across the street, Holberg's sprinkler waters his lawn, defying the drought regulations, and thinking he will fly under the radar during working hours. It's a long sprinkler connected to the hose, and it moves back and forth, making a thin arc of water that just catches the edge of the sidewalk, its dark wet stain almost defiant. In her rearview mirror, Lucy watches the water reach its peak, where, for only a split second, the law of gravity is suspended, and the water stands upright. At that moment, that split second moment, the upper layer of water catches the sun, and at that moment, that split second moment, there is a rainbow. A bloom of red, orange, blue and green that shines almost metallic. She watches it. Holds it. Owns it. The rainbow will be all hers until she looks away, if even for that split second, at which point the water will begin to tumble.

Once in her house, Lucy goes straight back to her bedroom, and straight into the closet, that one place in the world where the tragedy hasn't yet happened. Ordered just the same as the morning before she'd heard the news, when she'd gone in there for her brown dress and tights.

She reaches up and pulls down on the string. The light bursts on, but is somewhat dim and uneventful in the middle of a bright day.

Henry kept two shelves. The top one holds sweaters. They look like a table at a department store, with each one precisely folded, ordered by their thickness and seasonal purpose, and within that by their color. Unlike her shelves, which also try to maintain some sense of order, Henry had always been able to put his clothes back in the exact same place. It's impossible to imagine they'd ever been unfolded and worn. In contrast, hers always become a little off-center. Slightly shoved in. A little wobbly. The second shelf holds his pants and shorts. They too are arranged by style and color. Rows of shirts, slacks, and a couple of sports coats fill in his quarter of the rack, still in dry cleaner plastic, as if just delivered. Her therapist tells her she should keep the clothes until she is ready to take the next step, and Lucy always feels a little judgment in that, as though she clearly is doing something wrong, and the world is just extending her its limited patience.

But it doesn't work anymore. The closet no longer is her safe house. Those voices about burial services and bone chips and jazz concerts and legal strategies now echo against every wall in here, just as they do everywhere else. Suddenly, she can't stand the thought of living with Henry's clothes. It's now nearly impossible to see them as anything but memorialized shrines. "Son of a bitch," she screams, loud enough to reach Holberg's house across the street. "Goddamn, motherfucking, son of a bitch!" How is it that this last physical space of order and routine that could place her into the time before the attacks has crossed into the mess of the *after* of the shooting?

She steps out of the closet, trying to shut the door but it won't close, due to a latch that never quite catches in the strike plate.

Lucy runs out to the garage, wiping her eyes with the back of her hand, lifts the door, and in her arms balances a collection of dusty boxes of various sizes, bracing them down with her chin.

Back inside the closet, it is not Henry's clothes that she starts packing. Instead, she goes to her own shelves, and she scoops up the piles, trying not to disrupt the folds, and lowers each into the various boxes. She fills three of them. She repeats this with the contents of her dresser drawers, filling another two with socks, underwear, and T-shirts. And then, returning to the closet, she mashes her hanging clothes into three separate sections, lifting out each one and laying them on the bed, one on top of the other.

In less than an hour, all that is left are Henry's clothes. Still perfect. Still in place on his shelves.

Lucy carries her boxes out to the car, stacking a group of three in the trunk, and then draping the hanging clothes over them. She fills the backseat with the rest. She takes no pictures. No mementos.

Back in the house, before she leaves, Lucy drags her cello into the closet and puts it in front of Henry's shelves.

She drives down H Street to Alhambra, where she takes the on ramp onto 80. Merging onto 99 heading south, she turns off the news as it reports that nearly one thousand people have shown up for AG Hopkins's announcement on the east steps of the Capitol. Instead, she pushes in the disc of *Blue Train* that she'd finally burned the other evening. Lucy sets it to repeat.

She is flying past the exit to the COG. Past Stockton. Past Lodi. Manteca and Modesto. Through Fresno. Fields and billboards and quickie gas station and fast food stops. There are hardly any cars. An occasional trucker. Sometimes a family in a rental driving under the speed limit in the fast lane. But she's in no hurry.

The reeking pungency of the soil from the Central Valley farms overpowers her. For a moment it smells sweet until turning back into fetid waste.

She is driving toward where the shooting and the attack took place. But that is only a pull. Something gravitational and instinctual.

And maybe come tomorrow morning when she doesn't arrive for work on time, when it becomes apparent that she may not be there at all, maybe then Edith Franks again will call. Maybe then Edith Franks will remind her about the rules and systems and expectations that keep a complicated system in order.

Yes, maybe then Edith Franks finally will call.

But until then, Lucy will keep driving, until at some point she'll veer left, eastward. And then she'll drive until she can't drive anymore. And then maybe she'll take an airplane. A boat. A train.

BOOK THREE

EDGAR

THREE WEEKS AFTER Lucy bailed on the Jazz Therapy group, in the basement of the COG, Amy points a finger high toward the ceiling as the band rises to its crescendo, driving all the musicians to hold the final note one or two beats longer while the cymbals and the bass build and build and build, and then she looks at Edgar and the drummer, nods, and then drops her arm with full force, bringing *Blue Train* and six weeks' worth of work to a dramatic conclusion. As he lets the last note vibrate, Edgar notices the young woman in the very back, maybe mid-twenties, whose gaze is focused on him. He doesn't remember ever seeing her before.

There are about fifty people there. Mostly friends and family. A few people who Amy knows, and some staff from other COG programs. Amy had wanted to give it a nightclub feel, and thus had round tables brought in, with the folding chairs placed around the top halves of each one. She wanted candles for each centerpiece, but the building manager wouldn't allow it, a fire hazard. When he first came in, Edgar admired her ambition, but he still thought it looked a little like the arts & crafts room with the lights dimmed, not a jazz club.

The audience claps politely, fueled more by supportive pride than by true enthusiasm. Edgar bows when Amy's final introductions come to him. He scans the crowd, again noticing the young woman watching him.

During the reception, there are cookies: chocolate

chip and oatmeal; lemonade has been pre-poured in small milky plastic cups. Most of the audience hangs around, milling. Edgar lays his bass on the stage, and hovers near it. A polite expression on his face. He doesn't like this type of stuff. Everybody else seems to know someone. What little he can muster for these kinds of social situations he has to save for work, where he becomes King Bullshit. That is something to be stockpiled and stored. There's only so much in the reserve tank.

A wiry guy in shorts and a polo shirt, about Edgar's age, comes up to him. He introduces himself as a friend of Amy's. He tells Edgar it was wonderful, that the tenor sax really took it home in the ending bars. Edgar nods in agreement. What else can he do? The guy is here out of charity, and probably a little wary of being around all these head cases. Stepping away, the man pats Edgar on the back as though he's proud of him. It's meant to be inspiring but it comes out as patronizing. Edgar smiles, and draws his hand into an awkward salute that just falls limp.

Still alone, the young woman who applauded for Edgar stands near the rear wall, facing away from the room. Her cup of lemonade is on a folding table. She's gathering her long chestnut hair into a bunch and twisting it up in the back, while snapping on a jaw clip to keep her hair up and off her face.

Twice more, he glances her way. Each time he has the feeling she's just been looking, just before her eyes drop to study the floor.

He drifts away, thinking about an earlier moment tonight, near the end, where the alto sax and the tenor sax sailed into a single harmony, a long sustained note that bent and then slid into another. For just a few bars, Edgar forgot he was even playing bass or even listening to music, so swept into the emotion of that sonic moment that, for the first time in he didn't know how long, he experienced something pure and emotional without processing a single thought. It was frightening and exhilarating. Almost freeing.

Feeling a light touch on his upper arm, Edgar is startled back into the present. There she is before him. He hadn't even seen her coming across the room. Up close, there is nothing familiar about her. Shorter than Edgar, and about half his age, she stands on her toes and draws in closer, as though trying to see if she knows him. Her skin is clear, her eyes narrowed. She is pretty, in a driven kind of way. "Are you the bassist?" she asks.

He tells her, yes, that he'd played bass in the band tonight.

She raises her voice to be heard over the volume of the crowd. "So you are the regular bassist?"

He nods.

"From the beginning?"

"Maybe not the original. But for the last month or so, at least. That's regular, I think."

She lets out a long sigh, and this time touches his elbow. It's as though her whole body exhales at once. "You were my last hope," she says. "I was pretty sure I'd have to give up."

Edgar isn't sure where to look. He's suddenly afraid to look her in the eyes. He glances quickly around the room, and then back at her. It's all a little weird, this whole situation. He says, "Maybe I'm not *that* bassist."

"But you played with Lucy, right? Here. In this band."

"I really shouldn't talk about the others."

"But she played the cello with you, right?"

"Just for a week or so . . . I really shouldn't be . . ."

She repeats, "I was pretty sure I'd have to give up."

•

Over coffee, at the same booth where he'd sat with Lucy just weeks earlier, Edgar learns that Lucy didn't just disappear on the Jazz Therapy band, but that she disappeared on everything. The woman, Sarina, explains that she and Lucy worked together at the State Archives, and that they'd grown pretty close over the past year. But then one afternoon at lunch, Lucy walked out of the building. The guard at the security desk remembered Lucy saying she was stepping out to make a phone call. But she never came back.

Edgar says, "I didn't know where she worked. It never came up. I should have asked. Maybe paid a little more attention. I was just so pissed about how obvious it was she was being used, and, to tell you the truth, I think Hopkins's campaign already is starting to prove me right." He stops. Apologizes. Then he takes a small nicotine patch from his coat pocket, peels off the backing, and threads it through his sleeve, bandaging it on his upper arm. "Trying to quit," he says.

Sarina picks at something in the corner of her eye. "I only found you because I saw a listing for the concert in the paper, and Lucy had mentioned she'd made friends with the bassist. I thought I'd try. Hoping you knew something." She seems on the level.

"Have you gone to her house?"

"There's a light on in the bedroom. But her car is gone. And at first her phone rang and rang and rang forever. Now it gets a disconnected message. Nobody seems to know anything. Even at work they act like she just stepped out for a moment. It's so, so weird."

His eyes bore into Sarina. Her concern and determination are intoxicating, stirring up the feelings he'd been trying to rid himself of through the Jazz Therapy—the drive to not give up on finding Erin. Yes, it once overtook all aspects of his life. And, yes, in the end it only made him feel continuously crappy for not doing enough. But that tenacity never fully disappeared. At best, it only lay dormant. "We've got to find her," he says, clapping his hands. "We've got to make sure she is all right. Who knows where she could be."

Sarina backs up in the booth.

"Now your first duty, when you get to work on Monday, is to meet with your boss or someone who might know something." He can feel a familiar energy coursing through him. It's almost like a sting of adrenaline. "Maybe they don't even know there is cause for concern. I don't mean to go overboard, but she could be sitting in some hospital with no memory of who she is, for all we know."

"You really think so?" She lifts a napkin off the table and nervously dabs at her mouth. What little there is left of her lipstick smudges against the paper. It looks stained. She asks, "You really think that's a possibility?"

He thinks back to his brief conversation with Lucy at this very table, at the time so lost and turned around by her circumstances. Now she literally is lost, and what good are we as humans if we give up on the lost? How can we live with ourselves? "You're the one," he declares, "who said you were afraid you'd have to give up."

BRUSSELS. MUNICH. Orlando. Nice.

Istanbul. Kabul. Dhaka. Baghdad.

Nampala. Normandy. Damascus. Toronto.

Every day, it seems, a breaking news report. And every day, from his living room, Edgar watches it all unfold on the evening news.

It is a faceless enemy, these terrorists, almost exclusively represented by their horrific actions, their statements on social media, and the occasional video produced like a campaign by Madison Avenue for its most prestigious account, the people in it looking more like actors, posed and perfectly reactive. And it is that very facelessness and namelessness that is driving the US citizenry to question its own leadership, and its own leadership's ability to deal with an enemy that is more of a brand, rather than one built by named opposition leaders. It's that very line of thinking that can make someone as bombastic as Whit Hopkins appealing as a United States Senator. It's a thought Edgar has found himself having to squash when it creeps up minus the reason and the logic.

At home there only is one name that is known, and that name is Ryan Mohammad Khan. Ryan Mohammad Khan, who has been in custody since the Southern California attack. The hapless friend who phoned in breaking news accounts to the actual perpetrators, the semi-literate coward who was swept up into the idea of "doing something big," and had been discovered in front of his Xbox playing GTA with the very phone on his lap, no contents erased, no effort to hide or eliminate his tracks because he was too much of the village idiot (to quote a former acquaintance) to understand any complicity in participating in one of the deadliest and most brutal attacks on U.S. soil since 9/11. Regardless, Ryan Mohammad Khan, a twenty-four-year-old Iraq war veteran diagnosed with PTSD, has become the face of worldwide terrorism, still sitting in Victorville, and still awaiting trial.

First seeded through the TV news, cable shows, and talk radio, a movement has grown to ask why his trial has not yet taken place. They say the lack of any justice broadcasts a signal of our weakness to the rest of the world. And soon members of Congress have joined in, echoing their constituents and the pundits with those very questions, and demanding answers of the executive branch. More localized, AG Hopkins has been defending the work of the U.S. Attorneys, but blasting their Washington bosses for neutering the ninth circuit's good work in favor of their own failing political agenda—something he says the incumbent, his opponent, clearly endorses, if, by nothing else, her total inaction. Initially, the White House makes the argument that the U.S. Attorney's Office is proceeding with all the various steps one normally takes in our system of due process. The spokesman even makes a snippy remark that sounds remarkably like the president, saying, "This isn't *Law & Order*, folks. You don't solve, try, and convict in an hour."

But the calls only get stronger, Ryan Mohammad Khan only becomes more sinister, and even the White House recognizes the *optics* of the situation. Tonight's news covers the White House press secretary's announcement that the president too has been frustrated, and he has requested news reports that just hours ago from the briefing room, it was announced that the president too was frustrated, and he has requested an update from the Justice Department on the status of the case, and for a proposed timeline on both the state and federal trials. When the TV correspondent asks if the president supports the death penalty for Ryan Mohammad Khan, the press secretary merely states the president will be considering all updates and recommendations from the U.S. Attorney and the Attorney General, and that despite the president's own feelings about the death penalty, he will let the course of justice answer that question.

Edgar takes the remote, about to turn off the TV, but instead elects to flip to another channel. One where they are showing the same story from a completely different angle, with a slightly altered interpretation of the president's comment. The more he watches the clips of the press briefing, and the more he hears the various analyses and perspectives, the clearer it all becomes to him. It has nothing to do with the controversy surrounding the prosecution of Ryan Mohammad Khan. That is of little interest to Edgar. What does interest him is why no one seems to know that Lucy has up and disappeared.

EDGAR EXPLAINS THEY need a plan. He and Sarina are sitting in his living room on Monday evening, three days after the jazz performance. She's seated in the very chair where Mildred once sat nearly two decades ago. The sun shines on her back. Taken at the exact angle, and with her hair down and being partially blocked by the shadow cast by the curtain rod, Sarina can look just like Mildred. It's as though time has never passed.

Edgar tells her every minute is a critical minute. That already they've lost three weeks. But, he tells her, they need to keep quiet about it. "Otherwise," he says, "you can risk becoming the focus of all the attention, and the do-nothing judgmental people will make it about you."

She says it sounds like he has some experience in these matters.

"Live long enough," he answers, "and you'll get a crack at just about everything." It's as much as he'll say to her about his past. She doesn't need to get that in her head.

Sarina reports that this morning she followed through with Edgar's suggestion. When she called to make an appointment to speak with the big boss, the one she and Lucy had called Stache Man, she was told she should come up immediately. Find someone to cover the desk for her. She described sitting in his office as feeling like she'd shrunk three times, engulfed by the armrests. Most odd was that before she even said what she came to discuss, Stache Man opened the conversation by saying he was trying to figure out what was going on with Lucy.

"Those were his exact words?"

"He might have said he was concerned."

The boss knew they were friends. He said he'd seen them chatting many times in the foyer. And he knew that Sarina had helped Lucy in a personnel matter, when a former supervisor had been harassing her. This was a sensitive issue, he told her. Normally he wouldn't breach an employee's confidentiality, but he was worried. "He remembered that Lucy was approaching the year anniversary. And he also knew that Lucy had been in the midst of arranging for a burial plot, squeezing it in during her lunch breaks, and that he understood . . ."

"Wait. Wait, wait, wait." Edgar stands from the couch. He reaches a hand down to the back for balance. Even after all these years, a sudden movement can still make his knee go wobbly. "Did you say he said something about getting the cemetery plot?"

Sarina says that's right. "Among other things."

"Why would he know that?" Edgar asks. "How would he know that? I mean, did you?"

"I never asked her what she did with her lunch hour."

"And you said you'd never dealt directly with this guy before, and neither, I assume, had Lucy."

"Are you sure you've never done some kind of detective work?"

Edgar lowers himself back onto the couch. He feels trapped in an endless moment, one that began twenty-odd years ago when his sister, Erin, disappeared, followed by the beating, the memory issues, his failed search for her, and now Lucy. It's like he keeps flipping

151

channels, finding new programs and settings, only to realize partway into the show that they all have the same plotline and use the same script.

Sarina says, "You look bothered."

"It just doesn't make sense why he would know that, unless she's told him, but it sounds like he hasn't had any contact with her either . . . What else did he say?"

"He said for now they were quietly going to place Lucy on leave. If anyone asked, that was all I needed to say. He said she'd been through enough. It was the least the Archives and the state could do for the time being."

"And that's how it was left?"

"I did ask if I should call the police. And he said unless we had reason to believe something had happened to her of a criminal nature, or that we had evidence of a plan to hurt herself, that there was nothing the police could do."

"*People over the age of eighteen have a right to disappear.*"

"That's exactly what he said. How did you know?"

"Live long enough."

"Plus, he'd said, a call like that would generate media attention, and given everything Lucy has endured over the past year, that would be the worst thing that could happen—for people to think she'd gone over the deep end or something. Maybe she just needed time, he said. *Let's give her a little time without jumping to conclusions and ruining her in the public eye.*"

"Is that how you left it?"

"Pretty much. He just asked me to keep him informed if anything else popped up. To please let him know."

Edgar reaches for a throw pillow. He hugs it against his chest. "Don't tell him we're talking. No matter what, don't fill him in on anything we learn. I don't think we can trust him. Probably directly connected to Hopkins's campaign. This guy sounds like walking bullshit."

Sarina leans forward. Her voice lowers to a whisper. It's a little hard to hear at first, as a city bus rumbles by outside. She says, "I didn't tell him about her jacket that she left behind. That I took it home. I mean, there's nothing there really, but it seemed so private. And as much as he talked about wanting to preserve her privacy, it also felt like suddenly we were invading it, and somehow the idea that he might want something to do with her jacket seemed so invasive, as though we no longer would be helping her, but instead trying to catch her. Is that weird? That's why I kept checking at her house. Trying to phone. And then I tried to look for you. Do I sound weird to you?"

Edgar looks right at her, and he catches himself, about to call her Mildred. He pushes the pillow to the side, and it drops to the floor, near his slippered foot. With his index finger, he touches his temple, and tells himself to say her name when he speaks. To drill in and reinforce that this is not Mildred. This is not a replaying of the past, part of the betrayal that he still believes widened the gap of time that allowed his sister to disappear forever now. "Sarina," he finally speaks. "No, you don't sound weird. But everything else about this does."

She sits back relieved. "So what's our plan? You said we need a plan. What's the plan?"

•

Sometimes he questions everything he thinks he knows. Sometimes he thinks all of them might have been right—his mother, his doctor, his uncle. Maybe his head did take such a beating that it rearranged his memories and thoughts. In fact, he admits to that having happened to some degree. There were people and histories and relationships he had to relearn during the rehab period—not because he couldn't remember the specifics, but more that he couldn't piece together the various and sometimes disparate contexts.

Looking back, it did fit the definition of confabulation. The diagnosis could make perfect sense to someone observing him and cataloguing the pieces of evidence. And Edgar himself would also believe it if that memory of the news clip from the Trade Towers bombing wasn't so clear. It's not just the details of the news broadcast that he can recall, but it's also where he was sitting (on the edge of his couch with a bowl of red grapes on his lap), what the weather outside was like (a little cloudy but no threat of rain), and his state of mind (exhausted).

Later, in order to prove him wrong, his mother had Pastor locate a YouTube clip of that news report, and together they'd watched it on his computer, and together they'd seen the footage of a woman being carried out of the smoky garage. But there was no tangible indication of it being Erin. In fact, it was impossible to tell if the woman was old or young, white or black, tall or short, thin or heavy. It was chaos caught in a smoke-filled haze. But Edgar chalked it up to being secondhand footage, probably someone filming the TV with a video camera two decades ago, and then uploading and digitizing worn and grainy footage to a low-resolution stream. He knew what he'd seen.

But even after they worked him into a state of doubt, his mother and uncle, just when he might have relented, other incidents cropped up to confirm he wasn't damaged or paranoid. For instance, there was the jacket—a tan-and-black gingham checked overcoat of Erin's that showed up in a thrift store in Akron, Ohio eleven years ago, in which a California driver's license was found in the pocket, and when the new owner, a student at the University of Akron, dutifully sent it back to the central DMV in Sacramento, they mailed it to Mrs. Duncan's house like it was routine. Edgar tried to track down information in Akron, but nothing turned up. According to the local police, the jacket could have had a dozen owners in as many states. Edgar made several phone calls and drafted several letters trying to get the actual coat back, but it had long since disappeared, re-deposited back into the thrift system, and ending up who-knows-where.

In truth, being CEO of Duncan Distributors does and has bored him. Growing up, he'd had curiosities that extended far beyond his birthright. And he was on track in college to finding them. If his sister hadn't mysteriously disappeared, and if the attack on him never had happened, he believes he eventually would have been able to break free of his own destiny. But those two events collapsed family responsibility in on him. They nearly crushed him with the business and its legacy.

It doesn't mean he still doesn't question himself now and then. It's just that he always knows what the answer will be. Maybe a subset of the answer is *vindication*? That gives him a lift until he remembers it comes at the cost of his sister still missing after nearly twenty years.

•

The first part of the plan, Edgar says, is that he will check all the area hospitals. He cautions that it would be expecting too much for it to yield anything, still you want to rule it out. You never want to regret overlooking the obvious. Next he says he'll check with local cemeteries, since, thanks to the information Sarina got from her boss, Lucy apparently was making arrangements. He asks Sarina where Lucy lives, as she likely looked for a burial site close to home, unless there was a religious consideration. "All things being equal, most people prefer convenience. Easy access."

There is a vague memory from the papers of her being from North or South Carolina or someplace like that. What do we know about her family? Maybe Sarina can look that up?

She says it makes her a little uneasy to bother the family at this point. "I'd hate to find out that we unnecessarily worried them."

Edgar concedes the point. "In that case, then we should fix a date. A deadline. If we don't hear anything by that point, we'll be forced to contact them."

She says, "This is serious, isn't it?"

"Maybe there is something left in the pockets of that coat she left behind." Edgar kicks the pillow under the coffee table. "Again, you never want to overlook the obvious. Just in case. You never, never know."

Sarina begins rubbing her palms back and forth against her thighs. She makes smacking sounds, as though her mouth is dry. "We used to be so stupid together, Lucy and I." Her eyes start to water, and she stares off in the direction of his living room, the striped shadow over her becoming more pronounced with the sun shifting position. "How did we get here?"

Seated only a few inches from her, Edgar is tempted to stand up, walk over, and put his hand on her shoulder. But he flashes back to Mildred, and how he'd let her in. Trusted her. And how she'd ended up in collusion with his mother against him, and thus left Erin permanently disappeared. At this point in his life, he needs to resist all urges.

Sarina sits up straight, inhales a deep breath, and then exhales it slowly, closing her eyes and shaking her head. A strand of her hair slips out from her clipped bunch. She brushes it off her cheek. But it slips right back.

She says she's better now. "It all gets to me, you know. I was there when she first heard the news, then through the immediate aftermath, and now this. It all just throws me when I really think about it. When I stop and pause."

Edgar nods, letting her know he understands.

She reaches back and pulls off the jaw clip. Her hair falls down, longer and a little bit more frazzled than he might have expected. As she did the other night in the COG, Sarina then pushes it back, trying to gather all the stray hairs into a well ordered bouquet, and then tacks the hair clip back on. She puffs out a sigh, and says, "Okay. Back together now."

Edgar says, "Welcome back." To himself, he thinks that he can't rely on her for too much. She seems too emotional. Too invested. Too weak.

IT HAS BEEN a busy three days for Edgar, thus delaying the plans he'd made with Sarina on Monday. So far, he's only managed to call a few of the area hospitals in between meetings at work, each time spelling out Lucy's name, giving his, and leaving his contact information; as expected, each one came up empty. What he's really been trying to do is to get to the cemetery. His instinct tells him that the answer to her disappearance begins there, especially given the pointed comment Sarina's boss had made about a burial. But work at the distributorship has bogged him down. There is one longtime major account he is trying to save, while at the same time trying to negotiate the addition of another. It's important they both resolve positively, less so for the financial health of the family business, but more so for maintaining the reputation of Duncan Distributors, one that despite his inherent lack of interest in it, Edgar still feels compelled to foster and curate.

It's been a goddamn headache, is what it's been. The burden of maintaining a legacy.

In the early part of the last century, Edgar's grandfather had come west from North Carolina, looking for any kind of work, and through friends ended up loading trucks at a shipping dock by day and washing dishes at night in a restaurant in Old Sacramento. This was during Prohibition, and though the family rarely admitted it, the eventual outcome strongly suggests that Alban Duncan was keen on rustling up an illegal drink for anyone who could pay. The lore is that after

Prohibition Alban started up the distributorship that specialized in beer. Running it out of the restaurant where he'd worked, by himself he trucked bottles and kegs as far as he could drive. As he began a family, so grew the business into a family business—one Edgar's father took over, and that his uncle, Pastor, temporarily managed following his father's death and through Edgar's college years, the drifting nonprofit phase, and the subsequent rehab and recovery. It is a point of pride that they are the only distributorship remaining from the original seventeen that sprung up in the immediate aftermath of Prohibition, and now the largest in the region, including being the exclusive for several national brewers. And though Edgar can find himself caught up in the day-to-day dramas, when it comes down to it, his main goal is to ensure that Duncan Distributors remains a family business—only because he believes it may be the one lighthouse that his sister Erin still will be able to see from distant waters.

But today, close to a hundred years after his grandfather came west, Edgar is dashing off emails. Noting available days for meetings or phone calls that the receptionist can schedule, all while trying to get out the door. With Sarina having given him Lucy's address, Edgar has been able to narrow down the most likely cemetery that Lucy would have visited. And if he can just get a handle on whether she actually bought a plot, arranged for a burial date, or anything else specific, then at least he can better understand if she still is in the vicinity, coming back, or maybe gone for good.

Man, could he use a smoke.

•

The bright red Target sign fills his rearview mirror. He parks behind a golf cart, near the office building, a small stucco hacienda that looks designed in a WPA project, functional and compact, and yet with very precise flourishes of Spanish stylings near the roof line and over the windows and doorway. He is in the car he usually reserves for meetings with clients. The one with the leather seats. A layer of dust covers its metallic chestnut exterior. He only took the client car because it was parked nearest the front door at the warehouse. A matter of convenience, since by the time he came out, the temperature was hot beyond control, and the growing clouds had turned the sky almost nighttime dark.

Stepping out onto the thin macadam, Edgar first feels the wind before he hears it. He glances up to see the leaves of the giant oaks populated throughout the grounds fluttering and flapping. When you can see their bottoms, it is said, you can predict rain.

Beyond, into the cemetery, Edgar sees a woman kneeling at a grave, while another man in a small black Ford inches along the winding road, stops, and with the engine running, jumps out and runs three bouquets to graves in a similar vicinity. The man hops back in the car, drives another twenty yards or so, gets out, leaving the car idling, and repeats the process of laying flowers on designated sites. Then he gets in the Ford, sitting and talking on the phone.

Edgar keeps his hand on the door handle. His forehead dampens; he can feel his blue dress shirt sticking to his back.

He is very aware he is about to cross a line.

A man steps out of the office. Standing on the narrow landing, he wears a deep red polo shirt, untucked and hanging over the waistline of his chinos, baggy and loose. In his hand is a clipboard, and he stares at it so intently that he isn't aware of Edgar just feet from him. His hair is thick and dark, looking as though it is naturally mussed. And he wears the same mustache that Edgar presumes he's been wearing since he first grew it in 1973. He is big, naturally large, and his demeanor seems harried and rushed, brusque and impatient. But when he notices Edgar, his face softens, and revealed is a gentleness, one that understands the nature of the business he's in. He says hello, and asks how he can help.

Edgar says, "To tell you the truth, I'm not even sure I'm in the right place."

"We pretty much only do one thing here."

Edgar smiles. Dressed in his slacks and button-up shirt, and driving the client car, it occurs to him that he might look like a salesman. If nothing else, he certainly doesn't look like he is among the grieving. He drops his shoulders. Tries to look relaxed. "I mean," Edgar clarifies, "I'm not sure I came to the right cemetery."

The man steps to the edge of the landing, and turns his palm up. "And here it comes," he says. "Let's go inside. Between the heat and the raindrops, it seems like no one could ever possibly win." His voice is soft and soothing, a strange opposition to his physique and countenance.

Edgar follows him to the door. Before entering,

Edgar looks back once behind him, takes his keys out from his front pocket and clicks shut the locks on his car door. In the distance, the woman still kneels over the grave, and the bouquet man in the black car still talks on the phone, the windshield wipers clearing the glass.

Taking a seat behind a well-organized desk, the man motions for Edgar to sit. He reaches over a neat stack of papers, and introduces himself as Gary. His grip is firm, his palm rough and chapped with calluses. At first he hears Edgar as "Edward," until Edgar corrects him. And then he says that Edgar is lucky to have caught him when he did. "Pillar to post these days," he says. "And then post back to pillar." Leaning to the side he clicks on his mouse, and his olive green computer monitor comes to life, brightening up, revealing a startlingly bright screen that requires a password. "Let's see if we can't get you straightened out," Gary says, speaking with a deliberate patience for a man who has been running pillar to post.

Edgar shifts in his chair. Something seems a little off. He has the feeling that he should just get up and leave. Like maybe he is in too far over his head. Or that his mother's warnings may have been right, that the old injury might pop up and distort his sense of reality. But instead he forces himself to gather his strength and build his confidence, drawing on the same skills he learned from his uncle to close a deal with a new client. He looks Gary square in the eye, and he says, "It's not quite that easy."

"You'll have to give me a little more than that."

"It's actually someone I know. She's been planning a funeral, and I'm unclear if this is the spot." Edgar

163

explains that he can't reach her right now. But that he wanted to get started helping with the arrangements, and yet he just can't remember if this is the cemetery they discussed. He is lying so easily now that he almost sees his story as true. His mother would have a field day with that one. And then he blurts out Lucy's name, thinking that the public recognition of Lucy's name and situation will give him some credence.

Gary reaches over and shuts off the computer screen. His face is stone. It's what someone might look like if he could simultaneously be awake and asleep. He says, "Look, friend, I don't know what you're after. Maybe you're a reporter. An I-don't-know-what. But I also don't really care. All I know is that people need to leave that family alone. There's something called privacy, you know. They've been through enough." The gentleness in his voice has hardened along the edges. It's a little like a fist clenching. "Now I have to get back to work."

Edgar feels trapped between Gary's obvious suspicions and his own lies. He can only imagine the sickos and weirdos that might come stalking someone like Lucy's husband once word got out; some trying to get a scoop, others for a photo of where the grave might be, others goofing around like it's some kind of joke. He'd be pissed too. Edgar looks right at Gary. He says, "It's for good reasons. I'm asking for good reasons." Then he reaches for his wallet, takes out a Duncan Distributors business card, and puts it on Gary's desk. "Nothing to hide," he says. "Nothing to hide."

Gary spins his chair around until his back is to Edgar. He leans forward and picks up a pile of brittle

164

yellow invoices off the floor. He stays leaned over until Edgar stands, and makes for the door.

Edgar treads down the two short steps to the driveway, twisting between raindrops. It's turned unusually humid. In his pocket he fumbles for his keys, and manages to click the door open without seemingly finding them. To his right he sees the woman still by the grave, and the bouquet man five car lengths closer. Engine still running. And still talking on his phone.

Edgar starts his car, blasts the air conditioning, opening the vents so that it blows right on his face. His damp back sticks to the leather seat. He shifts into reverse, accelerates lightly, but the car lurches forward, nearly clipping the golf cart, forcing him to stop with a slight skid. Checking the dashboard, Edgar sees the gear is in drive. How had he mistaken it for reverse?

At the sound of Edgar's sudden braking, the woman at the grave has turned her head. He pretends not to notice, instead lifting his foot off the brake and slowly steering around the cart. It's a tight turn, but he is too nervous to try reverse again.

Wanting to help doesn't make you a sicko or weirdo, does it?

He's not one them. Is he?

Still, Edgar has to give himself a pat back on the back. He did manage to confirm that he'd found the right cemetery. Wasn't that one step closer to Lucy?

•

Mrs. Duncan wants to know why the U.S. Attorney's Office is calling her. She wants to know what Edgar has gotten himself into, and why he's involved her, as well. At this point in her life, should she need to remind him that she's an elderly woman? Sitting in the parking lot of Duncan Distributorships, a long mustard painted warehouse along a street full of warehouses that border I-80 for the easy shipping access, Edgar listens to his mother's message, after already deleting three of them sent over the hour he'd taken to go over to the cemetery. Mrs. Duncan says the reason she has had to call a hundred times is because he never phones back, and her only hope of speaking to him is the off chance that he'll actually pick up a ringing phone like a normal human being. But the U.S. Attorney's Office? She is hoping this is not a sign of regression, she says. She says she believed them to be well beyond that stage by now. That they'd passed through the eye of that needle. But she wants him to know she still retains power of attorney, and is chief officer in the family business. If he is putting himself into another mess like he started to last time, rest assured she will be exercising her powers.

Edgar notices that this message is verbatim with the other ones she left earlier, except with the addition that if he doesn't return her call immediately then she will be forced into next steps. This has now gone well beyond being a family matter.

Deleting it takes very little thought.

But what does stick in his craw is how exactly everything he considers with Lucy's disappearance is met as though it's been anticipated, if not expected. Sarina's boss seemed to know why she was there. At the cemetery, Gary immediately shut him down once he said her name. And before he even returned back to work, his mother was calling nonstop about the U.S. Attorney's office.

Behind him, Edgar senses movement, like a shadow or another storm cloud passing through. Quickly, he glances up in the rearview mirror, but only sees the empty parking lot, a quiet street, and the rails of the freeway.

Even with nothing there, he still feels watched.

That's what they want you to think, he thinks. You work hard and do your best just to keep the doors open, and then you realize that an open door means you've left yourself exposed. No one may ever actually be looking. But then again they might. Especially if they want to.

Just what they want you to think.

IT'S A SIDE story, but one that catches his attention on the evening news. The lawyers for Ryan Mohammad Khan have scheduled a motion to dismiss, noting in their brief that after a year of endless continuances by the prosecution, their client's basic constitutional rights have been violated. This interminable wait, they claim, is in violation of Khan's Sixth Amendment right to a speedy trial. The People counter by arguing that time and time again, the Supreme Court has relied on a balancing test laid out in *Barker v. Wingo* to determine what is and isn't speedy—measuring the length of a pretrial delay against other factors. In this case, they claim, any reasonable person would see that the balance is being perfectly weighted. In terms of specifics, the prosecution only will state that it needs the time for further preparation due to the complex and uncharted nature of this unique case. But any more than that will not be made public, in consideration of some of the sensitivities regarding national security, as well as documents that have yet to be declassified—or in some instances may remain classified. The defense counters that such evasiveness alone is clear evidence of prejudice suffered by the defendant from the delay. When the story cuts back to the studio, the anchor is speaking with a legal analyst who opens by saying there are valid points to be made from both sides, but in the end, she affirms, the case will go to trial, and, ironically this pretrial motion by Khan's attorneys will only further extend the wait for the defense. For the prosecution, she says, this is a win-

win, as they get more time to put their case together. The news anchor wonders what we are to make of the prosecution being unwilling to state what has been prompting the delay. She responds with their answer about the *unique nature of the case*, and then reiterates that part of the basis of the balancing test is that there is no set time limit, and that different circumstances need to be examined and understood in "balance" with the more literal aspect of a speedy trial. The anchor, still a little confused, presses. He asks, "Give us an example of what would be a justifiable reason for delay." The legal expert sighs. She shakes her head. "It really could be anything," she says. "From venue considerations to securing the presence of an absent witness."

AT ONE TIME it had been a new and fashionable neighborhood, planned and constructed east of the downtown area near the American River, with a flair of modern architecture that served as an antidote to the twenties and post-war bungalows that defined the city's last great building trends. In its nascence this subdivision claimed a new Sacramento, risen out of the shadows of a previous century that suddenly had seemed dingy and out of date. This was the land of split-level houses and raised ranches, with interconnected roads and cul-de-sacs, and circular driveways and carports and intercoms at the front door that led you into sunken living rooms and family rooms and sliding glass doors opening onto furnished cement patios. A world without nostalgia; there was no past to be redefined, it was a future being made in the present. These were the houses where each family had been both the discoverer and the first settler—a generation who mixed drinks at their bars and sang show tunes around the piano.

This is the neighborhood where Edgar grew up. The one he'd refused to return to after his sister disappeared, in protest of his family's denial and tacit complicity. The one he turned his back on following the beating, when he'd told his uncle Pastor that he'd rather hobble up two sets of stairs than lay around comfortably in "that emotionally abandoned mausoleum." It's been nearly twenty years since he's come back, even though he lives no more than ten miles away.

Such is the power of his mother's request.

When she'd got him on the phone, after going through the secretary at work with the charade of being a customer, she said they'd finally reached a nexus. He said he didn't think anything warranted him having to come over, it could all be handled by phone like everything else. She said it again: they'd finally reached a nexus.

Turning off of the tree-lined Fair Oaks Boulevard, and then driving down the main artery toward the river (from which all the streets of the subdivision splinter off of), Edgar sees the ragged and sagging present tense of the area. Once-pristine homes now have battered and rotted lawns. Driveways are filled with muscle cars and oil stains and plastic tricycles. And suddenly what had been the future all looks so temporary.

He slows the car before the stop sign, and then brakes, sitting there for an extra moment. He coaches himself not to give away that he has more anxiety about walking in and seeing Erin's old room than anything his mother might spring on him. She doesn't need one more edge. Especially since Pastor's death three years ago, it's just the two of them, both left alone but both of them left with each other.

At the corner, before he turns right onto his mother's street, Edgar notices that the old playground now houses a dented metal slide as its centerpiece; separated by a sand pit and a swing set with one swing that has been looped over the cross pole next to a companion that lolls back and forth eerily from the wind. At least the American River still flows just beyond it.

A winding cement path leads up to the door, bordered and landscaped by two paisley-shaped sections of white limestone pebbles, with a fish pond on the right, just before the entrance. Walking up, Edgar accidently kicks a stray pebble into the pond. It plunks, and the ripples look light compared to the dark, murky bottom. Skittish koi appear and try to scatter.

He reaches his right hand across his body and presses down hard on his upper arm, trying to push the nicotine by force into his bloodstream.

Mrs. Duncan cracks open the door before he can ring the bell. They stare at each other, Edgar and his mother. Zebra shadows are cast through the dark mahogany veranda.

Mrs. Duncan, a smallish woman, carries herself with a sophisticated matronly air. She always dresses as though expecting company, wardrobed in pressed tan slacks that flare at the bottom, a stiff-collared white shirt, and a paisley print hi-lo kimono that falls off her shoulders and hangs over her hips. Her hair is the same gray with black strands that she had last time he saw her, forever cut in a mid-length bob parted away from the forehead, sprayed and set at her hairdresser's. She stands in the threshold, blocking the doorway. Her right hand holds on to the inside of the door.

"This should be quick," she says.

"Don't rush on my account."

"I'm an elderly woman now. I don't have that kind of time anymore."

He asks if he should come in then.

She says she doesn't think it should take that long.

He should have felt relief at not having to go into that house. Stepping into the living room would have been like stepping into a memory come to life. Who would want to see the hallways where he and Erin once had run down? Or the table where he'd knocked over the Gump's vase, the anxiety of his parents' discovery so thick it had caused him to vomit? Who would want to stand in the area of the floor (nearly central to the living room, between the couch and the coffee table) where he and Erin had watched their father die? Not to mention, who would want to face the door to Erin's room, that portal to a deeper layer of memory? But strangely, Edgar experiences a sense of disappointment. It's as though his mother blocking the doorway means that she is controlling his power to deny the pain of the past, conversely keeping it more alive, and thus even more within her control.

Mrs. Duncan says there is one thing they need to be clear about. One thing and that is all. "Then you are free to leave."

When a large delivery truck of mulch starts backing up with its beep-beep-beep they both turn their heads to the street. Her right hand salutes against her forehead to block the sun. Once the truck crosses through the intersection, it turns left with a big blast of exhaust that forms two clouds dark enough that Edgar swears if they touched would make rain. Mrs. Duncan drops her hand, and then folds her arms over her stomach. She says, "I don't mean to be rude, but can we get this over with?"

Edgar nods. The once steely-eyed child, the fallen angel and the lone crusader, conjures up everything he has and stares his mother straight in the eye, knowing he might crack apart into a million little shards if he so much as looks away.

She says it's quite simple. "I don't know what you're

up to, and I don't really care to know. But what I do know is that I can't have you and our family business interfering in a federal investigation."

Edgar says he doesn't understand, and he really doesn't understand. Their family business? He's only trying to help find a friend because she might be in some danger. And he tells his mother that, trying to keep his bottom lip from trembling as his eyes moisten. "I'm only trying to help find her," he says. "I don't understand about an investigation."

"Since you are not dealing with reality, I will."

"This is a mistake. A total bureaucratic . . . Let me come in. We'll call whoever has been calling you, and we'll clear it up."

"As I said, I don't have this kind of time anymore. The U.S. Attorney's Office has made it quite clear to me that if this doesn't stop, then they'll be investigating the family business, going over all of our tax records, bookkeeping, and even suggesting they'll be reviewing any investments we might have made with foreign banks, and whether those involve supporting state sponsors of terrorism. It will be all over the news, and, as you probably can tell, that will force us to shut down—all over whatever you're doing. And that, simply, is not going to happen."

Edgar is stunned, playing and replaying everything that has happened since he met Sarina at the Jazz Therapy concert. Could just a couple of inquiries really cause so much concern? What was he in the middle of?

Mrs. Duncan backs up, taking one step into the house, blocking off Edgar from even a glimpse inside. She asks if they are understood.

"But what about Lucy?"

She shakes her head and rolls her eyes. Edgar knows what this must sound like to her, a twenty-year-old replayed question about Erin that she believes originated out of a brain injury, the effects of its condition she must be fearing have returned, but he wants her to know that this is different. That this is real. Immediate. He reaches out and grabs her forearm, a thin and brittle bone, and again asks about abandoning his friend.

Mrs. Duncan whips her arm, snapping his hand away. "I will have you removed first," she says, and then closes the door without a slam; the sounds of the latch closing like a bank vault shutting, the lock spun and the combination wadded, chewed, and swallowed.

•

Swinging a U-turn in front of the house, Edgar understands that this is the last time he ever will see his mother. With the closing door, she has disappeared herself from him, only ever to be in his life with the distance and automation of a bill collector. It should make him feel lousy. Break his heart and hurt his feelings and make him hate her even more. But instead he understands. She lost her husband too soon. Her daughter disappeared for reasons she puts on herself. And her son, her last family holdout, is someone who is forever angry at her, noncompliant, and probably permanently damaged. The one thing she'd been able to count on was that he could run the family business, and now it seems even that may be in jeopardy. When she isn't turning anguish into aggression and disappointment, it has to be so sad for her. She must feel just as alone. Her own expectations turned around and unrealized.

At the end of the street he pulls over in front of the old playground. It's a place where he spent so much time as a boy, left to his own devices and imagination. The playground at the river's edge was where he'd take off to when he needed to be alone to contemplate ideas, make discoveries, manage heartbreak, and make his vision of the future—one in which he'd always think up ways to deal with the world on his terms.

But now he's a torn man. Will he risk everything and continue to search for Lucy? And if he does, and if his mother does remove him from his job, or the feds actually shutter the business through harassment, will he lose the beacon he's kept lit for Erin?

He gets out and crosses the yard, fingers brushing the steel piping of the slide as he passes by it, trying to find that boy inside who came here by instinct.

Down a slight slope from the playground the old trail leads to the rocky shore of the American River. It's a short incline along a path carved out by years of feet trampling over the orange and dusty dirt and breaking down the weeds until they just refused to grow in that spot anymore. On both sides are littered beer bottles and crumpled cigarette packages and open potato chip bags and an occasional spent condom. Towering above lords an infantry of giant pyramided transmission towers that hold and direct ropes of power lines.

A few steps down the trail brings a rocky beach; it's always been tough to walk on. Either the rocks will shift or they can be mossy and slippery. In between them are shards of green glass that through the sunlight look sharper and more strategic. Negotiating the stones takes a focused assiduity given the weakness of his knee.

At the water's edge, Edgar kneels down and scoops his hand into the river. The water feels as cool and pure as he remembered, with a slightly sweet smell of algae. Then he stands and walks a little farther downstream until the American starts to bend. In his memory, he could walk forever along the bank. But now it seems to be impassable. The trail vanishes into a curve, giving way to a ridge of yellow stalks and dusty green shrubs.

Did the path seem longer when he was a boy?

Up ahead he hears girls giggling in the bushes. He figures them to be drinking or smoking, like he and his friends always did. They quiet when they see him. Both look to be about sixteen and they have identical haircuts with the same red streak highlighted across their bangs. In their nest are no visible bottles or cans. No smell of smoke. The girls just are hanging out. Talking. Killing time.

Edgar says hello, and they both give a little wave and a singsong hi.

He asks, "Can you still keep walking down here?"

One of them says, "It totally narrows," and the other nods in agreement, and says, "Really, really super narrow."

Edgar studies the river and the way it seems to disappear. He can sense its presence and he knows that it continues on, but from this vantage point once it takes the curve there only are weeds and power lines.

He says, "Well, I guess I'd better head back then. Leave you two alone out here, doing whatever you were . . . Seeing how there's nowhere to go here anymore.

Not like it used to be, that's for sure."

"It does get narrow."

"Super narrow."

Making his way upriver, he looks at every stone before stepping on it. They seem a little looser on the way out. Precarious. More prone to a simple misstep.

What's he going to do? He still has no idea. No further sense of clarity. Each possibility is both the wrong and the right answer.

From behind, the girls break out into a hysterical laughter. One of them says, "Oh my God." And the other says, "That was so weird. Maybe the weirdest thing ever. Who could imagine anyone would ever find us here."

Alongside him he can hear the water babbling along the rocks on the shore. In the distance he can make out traffic, and as he comes under the power lines he can hear the electricity crackling and it makes him think of the thousands of lives that are being lived at that very moment. And still floating in the light breeze that has come up is the girls' giggling, a bread crumb trail left just for him.

Edgar thinks to himself that at so many points in our life we just want to disappear and be lost, but only on the condition that eventually we again will be found.

THE EVENING NEWS IS reporting that the judge in the Khan terrorism case has sided with the defense. Sources are confirming that he has set a start date for two weeks. Given the defendant's right to a speedy trial, the judge is not persuaded that the government needs any more time than it already has taken. Critics already are attacking the president and his Justice Department. They say that Ryan Mohammad Khan should have been tried by military tribunal, and that he should not be afforded any constitutional rights. On the broadcast, it gets pointed out that Khan is an American citizen, and he did serve in the American military. And, as the president is quick to note in a White House statement via his press secretary: "To those who think otherwise, I want to remind you that we are a nation of laws and due process. These other ideas that are floating around—well, we're better than that." A rebuttal by a retired general says that this was an international war crime, and therefore Khan should be treated as an enemy combatant—this is a military issue. At this point, some legal experts predict that the government may have to look at taking the death penalty off the table if they want to see any success with this trial. If so, it could end up being a legal blunder for the history books. Not to mention a stain on the president's legacy and his battle to combat global terrorism. But the U.S. Attorney's Office has issued several statements to the contrary, denying that they will no longer be seeking the death penalty. They insist that the case is as airtight as it ever has been.

The prosecution's only concern is the matter of time, and they continue to press on that, first appealing the ruling, and then pushing it to the media, hoping that public opinion will apply the necessary pressure for another continuance. The judge isn't having any of it. He's not buying the classified-declassified argument. Appeal denied. *So, what is it?* the news anchor asks. The network's judicial correspondent says the prevailing opinion among court watchers is that the prosecution still is trying to track down some key piece of evidence that they must believe is vital to the case. All any of the experts can do is to speculate; at this point, no one knows what they are after.

Except Edgar. But he has been muted.

That Lucy's disappearance is key to the trial is not in question. Rather, it is the relationship to it. The fact that the U.S. Attorney's Office is threatening him and the family business suggests that they too are flummoxed by her disappearance. But at this point, two things seem pretty clear to Edgar: one, that based on the interaction at the cemetery, it would appear that Lucy is alive and still managing her life; and two, that the prosecution has no idea where she is, and therefore it does not want the slightest leak that she may not be a cooperative witness. (Not to mention how that might reflect on Whit Hopkins's campaign rhetoric.) But what is not clear to Edgar is if he's seen as a threat because his search is distracting the case, or if they think he may be abetting her.

Meanwhile, Sarina keeps calling him. Sarina keeps leaving him messages. And he doesn't return them. He doesn't do anything. And it's not that he doesn't want to. It's not that he doubts her concern, or doubts her allegiance to her friend. The truth is that Edgar is scared shitless. The past few mornings since he was summoned by his mother, he has driven into work constantly checking the rearview mirror for people following him. Coming into the office, past the secretaries and salespeople, he wonders how they see him, if they note a trace of fear in him—that little hesitancy in his step, the downward gaze when he can't manage to hold eye contact, that he is taking meetings at an accelerated pace, sending out email after email about cultivating their longtime accounts and not just taking orders, and that he appears a little distant in their weekly strategy meetings. If they were to notice, would they, like his mother, conclude that Edgar's nervous behavior means he's snapped again, and more importantly, that the business is failing?

Surely, they recognize something.

What they wouldn't know is that he's had his first confrontation with the Hard Power. Even though he chased bureaucracy and authority when he insisted that people deal with Erin's disappearance and the obvious connection of the Trade Towers bombing, he never really had been responded to in any kind of serious way. Now the Hard Power has answered him. It has stood toe-to-toe with him, and then taken a step toward him. It has threatened not to walk all over him, but to steamroll him and everything that came before him—erasing his family legacy, their name, and any hope of their future.

He has no idea what to do. And that, Sarina, is why you are avoided.

The Hard Power has won. It has spooked him.

Terrified him. Made him imagine the loss. Gotten in his head. Paralyzed him.

He has to decide what to do. He can't continue on like this.

Are they really willing to ruin him to keep from ruining their case?

He leans towards giving in to the Hard Power. Surrendering directly and forthrightly. Put on their uniform. And then, maybe then, they will let him be and leave Duncan Distributors alone. Only then would he be assured that the light could continue to burn for his sister Erin, wherever she may be wandering.

But what would it mean to sacrifice Lucy to the Hard Power?

He suspects that in order to preserve their death penalty case, the Hard Power's biggest concern is that it not be known that she has disappeared. They don't give a crap about her well-being. In fact, he's starting to believe they'd rather have her far, far away instead of fucking up their case. The problem in reaching any conclusions about the best thing for him to do is that he has no idea what she wants. But he just can't believe anyone wants to be lost forever. He can't fathom it. And if he succumbs to the Hard Power for the purpose of making sure the door is open for Erin, he knows he is making certain the door always remains closed for Lucy.

A DORMANT INSTINCT overtakes him the moment he wakes up. Against his drawn shade blasts the brilliant orange of dusk. Edgar feels like a man on his deathbed, racing the clock to ensure his legacy and mission doesn't disappear with him. His father had always told him not to need anything from anybody. Then you'll never be subject to them. Maybe if he can just find Erin now, he won't be caught in this no-man's land of a decision. Then there will be nothing the feds can hold over him.

He pushes off the covers, kicking the last end of the sheet to free his feet, and without grabbing his robe off the hook, he ambles into the living room in only his boxers and t-shirt, and in the pine credenza against the back wall, opens a drawer that in rehab he'd claimed to have emptied long ago. Digging under a pile of old bills, newspaper clippings, and appliance manuals, he pulls out a paper-clipped packet of handwritten notes. Flipping back past the middle, as though he knows the order of the clutter by heart, Edgar finds a list of New York City hospitals among his collection of papers about the Trade Center bombing. He snatches a pen off the counter, grabs an envelope from yesterday's mail to write notes on, and then starts dialing the telephone, thankful for the time difference, knowing that the East Coast hospitals will be well open by now.

With the first call, to New York Presbyterian, Edgar feels the old sensations coming over him. That full sense of conviction. A layer of hope, with, at its core, a feeling of elation. But he also hears those continuous whispers that not only reinforce the impossibility of actually tracking down Erin, but that also remind him of his foolishness and of Dr. Merman's diagnosis of confabulation due to the head injury. It's as though he hardly can breathe, waiting for the operator to answer; and, although he knows it is completely improbable, he half expects to recognize the operator's voice, and for her to know his, saying they've been wondering why it took so long for him to phone. That they've been waiting for him.

A momentary shot of expectation rattles through him when after the third ring a woman picks up. Her voice *is* familiar, until he remembers that operators are professionally interchangeable, never meant to show their own personalities. Edgar asks to be transferred to medical records, following the script like an aging actor reviving his greatest role—every word known by heart, the delivery so familiar as though it's someone else speaking it, and yet a hair overdramatic, the naturalness of the part having been replaced by *acting*.

It doesn't surprise him to hear there is no record of anyone named Erin Duncan having been in the hospital during the timeframe given by Edgar. Nor is there anything noted that he'd once called, asking them to list him as a potential next of kin should she turn up. The young man in medical records, likely born when Edgar first had inquired, says he doesn't even believe they have a system for that; most people go through the police. He adds, "Maybe you reached a sympathetic nurse or someone when you originally contacted us. If you can remember a name, I could try to run it down." Edgar quickly glances over his notes. There was no name. And, if he is honest with himself, there was no such offer; it was only a simple declaration that he'd made, met with some muted affirmation intended just to get him off the phone. *It's okay*, Edgar says, *never mind*. The young man, somewhat apologetic at not being able to provide the service, adds that the computer systems and software have changed over the years, especially *since then*, and it's always the value fields for medical non-essentials like "other notes" that never transition well.

Since then.

That's the phrase that sticks in Edgar's head.

Since then.

It is reinforced when he dials Roosevelt Hospital, only to find out that is has been renamed Mount Sinai West at some point over the past couple years.

Since then.

•

The first time around, coming up empty had undone him. It had driven the wedge between the family. Dictated his life. Certainly ruined his friendship with Mildred (even though he always understood its basis had been her guilt about feeling responsible for the beating and subsequent injuries). It also had solidified his worldview of living in a culture that doesn't think twice about betrayal, all in conjunction with a society that devalues loyalty. The only plus side had been that it ratcheted up his commitment to leading a life of loyalty. He'd stayed loyal to his sister. To his employees. Even in some convoluted way to his family. He always acted on behalf of his Uncle Pastor when he'd been alive, gave his mother the necessary distance she needed to live with some dignity, and, of course, he maintained his father and grandfather's legacy through the business. Still, the one area he is letting himself down on the loyalty front is with Sarina.

Edgar straightens the papers, tapping the edges against the table, and then rises to return them to the credenza and back under the menus. He is tempted to take them straight to the kitchen garbage bin, but he's afraid he might inadvertently let go of something important. After all, it wasn't that long ago that Erin's license was found in that thrift store jacket in Akron, Ohio—the coat he regrets never being able to locate. That's all that is holding him back. Otherwise, he is quite prepared to trash this part of the search. It's time to give up on the hospitals.

Since then.

Sliding the pages into the drawer, he notices a note in Mildred's handwriting. He half-remembers it, something about a doctor's appointment and making sure to ask about a medication she'd heard of that might help with the headaches, and to ensure it is covered under his plan, and if not to ask about a generic. The content is of no interest anymore, nor is the nostalgia of seeing her name signed with the large swirled M that always reminded him of a short mountain range with two steep peaks.

Seeing Mildred's note recalls the deep, deep sense of betrayal he'd felt when she'd conspired with his family to get him into the rehab center. But now, with distance, he has come to see it from her perspective, and from that long view it was an act fully steeped in loyalty—an action meant to help him because she honestly believed no one was helping him at the time. Mildred understood his family had been managing him solely for their own ease. She understood Edgar needed to get back on track again for his own well-being, not theirs, and that there were systems and supports for making that happen. Only now does he get that Mildred wasn't conspiring with his mother; rather, she was conspiring against her.

But he'd cut her off. Shut her down, even when she'd tried to follow up. One time he had seen her out on the street, a zillion years later; and even then, years after the fact, when all should have been forgiven, he avoided making any contact with her, like a jilted teenager, still wounded and raw.

•

It only takes a couple of minutes to find Mildred on the internet. When he'd last seen her on the corner across from the Capitol, Edgar had taken her for a lobbyist or a chief-of-staff, such was the posture and official countenance she displayed. And he wasn't too far off. In fact, she heads a project within the California Energy Commission—investigating renewables and something or another. Seated at the computer, his thighs sticking to the seat, he studies the thumbnail photo of her, posed and textured like all the other government photos.

A complete stranger on the page, yet undeniably Mildred.

He has no need or inclination to apologize or to make restitutions. But he does have a yearning to know what he should do in his current dilemma. Looking at the photo of Mildred he's drawn back to her confidence, commitment, and loyalty. She was unfettered in her support for him. She sacrificed for his good. And Mildred always understood the system.

The longer he stares at her picture, the more he becomes convinced that he needs her counsel to find and make the right decision.

•

Entering the lobby of the Energy Commission, Edgar is aware of being observed. It is relatively quiet and somewhat sterile, almost black and white, particularly unexpected considering the brightly rich, colorful ceramic murals covering the exterior on the Ninth Street side.

He is acutely aware of being only a few blocks from the State Archives, knowing Sarina certainly is there, and probably also being tailed. That is the kind of shit he needs out of his mind when trying to make his decision. It is too persuasive.

At the security desk, the guard opens his binder, flipping pages back and forth, and asking Edgar twice to spell Mildred's name and then his name, before phoning upstairs. It's a quick call. One that appears routine and businesslike. But Edgar can hear the awkward pauses. He can sense the silence before and after the guard repeats Edgar's name into the phone. And without relaying any of the content, the guard points to the opposite end of the room. "Take a seat," he says. "She says she'll come down."

As he waits, it occurs to Edgar that Mildred probably

knows something. If the U.S. Attorney has been looking into him, surely they have thumbed through his past, and, if so, it is perfectly reasonable to assume they may have contacted Mildred. And suddenly he feels the fool. The embodiment of Oswald's patsy.

The numbered lights on the elevator bank are descending. He stands up, still with time to leave.

The guard looks across him to him, nods, and holds up an index finger, indicating it only will be a minute more.

Edgar doesn't sit. He meanders around the edge of the building, staying near the door, and trying to shelter behind a freestanding poster that celebrates the wind power generated from the coastal waterways.

Hospitals. Cemeteries. More hospitals. Police stations. And now he's here. The story of his adult life: chasing hope. Nothing really ever changes.

From behind the poster, he sees all the elevator doors in the bank open at once, one-two-three in order, and out of the third comes Mildred, wearing a coffee-colored linen dress, with her shoulders draped by a light blue cotton sweater. Despite twenty years of aging, and a maturation of style, this Mildred looks more like the old Mildred than his memory had memorialized. With a kind of efficiency, Mildred marches straight to the desk, and she bends slightly at the waist, as though avoiding having to raise her voice, and the security guard points in Edgar's direction.

"Edgar," she calls across the room. The voice is so familiar that it could be coming from his own head. And when she says his name again, Edgar has the sensation of watching a dubbed movie. Voice and actor not quite matching.

God, does he wish he'd left.

He puts his hand out, but she grips both his shoulders and pulls herself in a for a hug. Still thin, she now feels solid. And her breath against his cheek is more alive than anything he's known in a long while. He's never felt so old. Almost embarrassingly so.

She says she figured she'd never see him again. This is quite a surprise.

He explains how he found her on the internet. "Nothing weird, though," he assures. "Nothing weird. I just got to thinking was all."

She motions him to sit on the bench, and she takes a seat beside him. Her knees press tightly together. "I've wondered," she says. "For a long time I've wondered." And then she offers a preemptive apology, explaining that it is a very hectic day, and that she has a meeting at the top of the hour.

"I never expected."

She says, "This sure is a surprise. We were just babes in the woods then. And looks at us now."

Edgar glances up at the clock. There only is a matter of minutes until the top of the hour. And while this is his moment to explain why he actually came, to tell his story, and to seek her wisdom, he can't manage to say anything. It's as though he's gone mute.

She says, "I never wanted to intrude. That's the truth. My explanation . . . I just feel as though I need to say that. That's all."

Edgar nods. He sees her check the time, and then she shifts restlessly. It is a strange sensation, fully and completely visceral, in which he actually feels the

190

moment slipping away, something akin to the giant tug of a vacuum, or the force of a drain pulling the water downward.

She rubs her palms along her thighs. She says it was rude of her. She says, "I shouldn't have just come down knowing I only had a few minutes. It would have been better to schedule something when there was more . . . But when I heard your name."

He says, "It's okay. Really, it's okay."

"And I didn't even get to hear what you've been doing these days. How you are."

"It's, you know."

"Maybe we can catch up properly?" she asks, starting to rise. "Maybe even with a Zelda's pizza, if they're still in business."

Edgar stands with her. He says, "There is so much to say, and yet nothing at all seems new."

She says to look at the time. Making him walk with her to elevator, she confirms that they will connect soon.

Edgar tells her absolutely, even though he knows it likely will never happen; agreeing to that is nothing other than a smooth conclusion to what had been a jagged ending.

As she backs in to the elevator, she says to Edgar, "I'm glad you found me." He watches the doors shut, and hears the bell above it chime. He doesn't look up to see the ascendant floor numbers lighting.

On the way to his car, Edgar detours over and up a few blocks to the corner of the Archives Building. He just stands there for a moment, surveying it. Taking it in. And he thinks that although he never got to ask Mildred his question, in a way, through her reinforcement of his expectation of her loyalty, he found his answer.

A group of kids chatter and scream at the Archives Plaza rail stop. Looking over, he focuses on the entrance, imagining Lucy coming out its doors and walking into the day and disappearing as though passing through a curtain.

Not everyone who is found, he thinks, meant to become lost.

•

He can't wait. He knows he should. He knows that any urgent need to do something is best met by pausing and waiting. He learned that years ago at the rehab center. The more you want something, the more time you need to consider and evaluate. He spins around in his office chair, too distracted by what he wants to do. It's impossible to focus on work, despite a pending meeting that he should be prepping for, as well as beginning to review the monthly billings. The biggest argument for waiting is that he really shouldn't make the call from the office. Conflating his business and his personal life is at the very heart of the conflict. But such a detail makes no difference. Because he just can't wait.

Belinda knocks on the door and pokes her head around the threshold. Kind and committed, Belinda worked for his father, although in a lesser role straight out of high school, coming on just a month before he died. Although only about ten years older than Edgar, she's always seemed as though she's part of an entirely different era, almost like one of his grandparents' generation. Lately, though, it seems as though they've finally caught up with each other.

Belinda wants to let him know that the two o'clock conference call has been pushed back to three. He thanks her, and asks her if she can run the inventory list once more. He wants to be as up-to-date as possible. Once she returns from lunch, Belinda says. Then she's all his.

When she leaves he turns to his computer, and looks up the ninth circuit, the U.S. Attorney's Office for the District of Southern California. He writes down the telephone number on the back on an envelope. Then he closes out the window, and shuts down his computer for good measure. You never know how they might track you.

Now he just has to wait through lunch, and then make sure to call between one and two.

His mother would say it was the injury from the brain doing all the thinking. If Pastor were alive, and word got out, Edgar is sure as shit that he'd be being hauled out to the rehab center in the pickup; or else, more than likely, to a hospital with doors that locked. He'd try to argue that it is what his mother wants, even if they don't see eye to eye on the intended outcome. That it's based on a rational conclusion drawn from seeing Mildred. An epiphany that alit out of what had seemed to be a hazy moment. Can't they see it's about keeping hope up for Erin? But his mother never would have it. Even when he'd argue that thinking such thoughts is further evidence of his own lucidity. He can't be crazy if he's parsing it out so clearly.

As he waits, Edgar checks the news on the web. There are plenty of opinion pieces about the state of the Ryan Mohammad Khan case. Nearly every one he reads is of the belief that the U.S. Attorney's Office is either having trouble with a key piece of evidence, or else they are straight up bungling the biggest slam dunk since the O.J. Simpson trial, and staring down the barrel of a similar outcome. It reinforces and strengthens the decision for what he is about to do. Show them that they have a partner, and move on to their side.

At exactly one o'clock, Edgar dials the 855 area code, slowly typing out the rest of the numbers. As the phone rings, he has yet another feeling of being on a precipice—only this time, instead of crossing into some other place, he believes it will be a downhill slope back into a safe and comforting valley.

Adopting as stern and as professional tone as he can muster, Edgar tells the receptionist he'd like to speak to the Honorable Margaret Kelly. He wonders if the receptionist can hear the quiver in his voice. He's never been so sure and so unsure of something in his life.

She tells him that Mrs. Kelly is not available. However, she can try ringing one of Mrs. Kelley's law clerks. He tells her no, that he really needs to be in touch with Mrs. Kelly herself. The receptionist's voice lowers. It's a gear she's clearly been trained for—diffuse a situation by staying calm, but keeping firm. "I can connect you to her voicemail, if you'd like," she says.

Edgar thanks her. It's to be expected. He knows they don't just put you through to the boss. But, given the news, he does believe his message will be heard.

Mrs. Kelly's recorded voice is firm. It has a hint of compassion with a heavy dose of law and order. At the beep, Edgar states his name and gives his phone number. And then he says he's calling regarding the disappearance of Lucy, explaining she is a friend, adding that Mrs. Kelly must already know that, and that while he doesn't know where she is, he is at their service in any way that can help. He repeats his name and phone number, and then slams down the phone, as if that is what makes the call permanent.

He heaves a sigh so deep that he almost starts to cry.

He doesn't know what will happen. If they'll even phone him back. If he's helped or betrayed Lucy. He just doesn't want to have done her in. But at least he does know that from this moment, every day forward, he can go into Duncan Distributors with a greater sense of relief—relief at having kept the doors of hope open for Erin.

IT'S A PACKAGE in front of his door.

He'd been sitting on his couch, polishing his bass, readying it for another run at Jazz Therapy. Amy had made the appeal by phone. She said he was her bottom; she was counting on him for the next session. He'd heard rustling, first in the hallway, and then right outside his front door. When it was followed by quick scuttling that faded down the steps, he pushed the bass aside, propped the neck against the couch, and went out to look.

He carries the box to his dining room table. It's standard sized, brown and reused, bent at the side and creased along the flaps, with his name written in marker over the scar of a torn-off mailing label. The box is so light that it might as well be empty; and though sealed, it is taped with thin strands of Scotch tape, like something from a desk dispenser.

Edgar places it on the table, and then rushes over to the window, looking down on the street. Maybe he can still catch a glimpse of who left it. The green in the park radiates brilliantly on a rare sun-filled fall day. A few people stroll through. An old man sits on a bench reading the newspaper, kicking away pigeons that dare too close. But there is no one who is familiar to him. No delivery trucks. Nor is there anyone who seems to be lingering or watching for him.

He should be cautious, he knows. Maybe even with a healthy dose of paranoia. But despite no reply to the message he left with the U.S. Attorney's office last week,

Edgar has felt more at ease. He wants to believe they now have an understanding.

In fact, since that call, all has been quiet. The phone has stopped ringing; he's heard from neither his mother or Sarina. Even news of the pending trial has slowed down. The nightly news reports, bored by the petty back-and-forth between the legal teams, have gone dormant until the trial actually gets set to start. At the very least, it assures him that Lucy is maintaining safely, wherever she may be.

It might be overstating it to say that a weight has been lifted off his shoulders, but at least it doesn't feel quite so heavy.

Back at the table, Edgar turns the box in slow circles, sizing it up, like a child trying to deduce his Christmas present before opening it. But he has no clue what it is, who left it for him, and why.

The tape is so thin that he doesn't need scissors. It peels right off, and the top flaps bounce up. Pulling them open, he sees a note on top. It is typed, a single-spaced paragraph, and at the bottom is a signature in hard blue ink—one name, *Sarina*. He plucks it out, noticing just below it is a piece of lime tissue paper. Balancing himself on the back of a chair, he brings the note up to the light, where the paper takes on a bluish hue. It reads that she knew he wanted to see this, and she hasn't been able to reach him (*I'm sure you've been really, really super busy*), but here it is, and no one else knows they have it, and whatever he wants to do with it, she'll go along with it. She ends by saying to be in touch when things settle down.

He drops the note, and lets it float down to the

tabletop. Then he straightens it out, and flattens it with his palm.

Without removing the tissue paper, Edgar dips both hands into the box.

Out the living room window, it's as though the whole valley has frozen for just a moment. The engines, the horns, the chatter. Even the sun takes shelter behind a cloud.

His fingers pinch a soft fabric that he pulls upward. The lime tissue paper blooms out, turning to a darker green. Like a magician's trick, the garment keeps unfolding and unfolding and unfolding.

Edgar immediately recognizes the gray overcoat as the one Lucy left behind at her desk the day she disappeared. It's just as he pictured it from Sarina's mention of it when they'd first met. In his hands it feels both heavy and light. Light, in that it is a small size, with thin and shiny fabric; but heavy in that it seems to carry all of Lucy in it, spirit and form.

He walks it straight to the bedroom closet. Holding the coat away from him, he slides open the door, and with his other hand, knocks his good corduroy sport coat off the wooden hanger, and then slips Lucy's jacket on to it. He adjusts the ends of the hanger into the shoulders, straightening them, and then suspends the coat from the top of the door.

Looking at it, Edgar no longer sees it as a jacket or an object, instead, he sees a full form; even when he rifles through the pockets and comes up with a bunch of nothing receipts and drops them on the floor, it is as though he has frisked her or something, keenly aware of his intrusion.

Taken together, it is spooky and reassuring.

Backing up, without ever taking his eyes off the hanging jacket, he stops at the edge of his bed, and then sits down. When he thinks back to his search for Erin, and to helping out Sarina in the search for Lucy, he realizes he has never had anything tangible. Everything has been based on a memory or an intuition or an inference. That's why he'd wanted Erin's Akron, Ohio coat so badly. Things from the past (photos, childhood tchotchkes, books, and such) always felt archived and historicized—they had little to do with the Erin that was out there now. He'd been after something that still carried her aliveness, not her memory. It was the same logic that made him swipe his father's reading glasses following the funeral, allowing him to see the world with his father when he looked through the lenses.

Now he has Lucy's coat. And through it he sees the lives of all those closest to him who have disappeared. He sees his father. He sees Pastor. Lucy. Erin. He even sees his mother.

The sun is coming back out. With the room lightening, the off-white walls take on a yellowish texture like a freshly painted fresco just drying.

He will sit there until the sun goes down and the room turns dark.

And when it does, he will stand up, go into the living room for his bass, and, as to not bother the downstairs neighbors, he will finger the notes of *Blue Train*, closing his eyes and gliding through the intro, in his head hearing the cello bow note-for-note with him, swaying until the horns ease in, moving through the improv until landing back on the theme and thus ending a playing session that brings him a sense of calm.

Two hours later he'll go to bed, noting how the gray overcoat fades away after he shuts off the light. When he wakes up in the morning—too early in the morning—and the coat still hangs there, a spot of sunlight stained across the breast, he will not turn on the news and hear anything about Ryan Mohammad Khan, and he will not head straight to Duncan Distributors, and he will not think of Duncan Distributors as any place symbolic; instead, he will send Sarina an email thanking her for the coat and adding that they need to get back to their plan. Next he will go to his kitchen drawer, pull out an emergency pack of smokes he's hidden behind the silverware tray, tap one butt out of the box, go into the dining room, sit at the scarred table, and light it up. And then he will reach for the telephone, and he will dial familiar numbers, and when familiar voices answer them, he will say, "My name is Edgar Duncan. Several weeks ago someone I know disappeared, and I want to rule out that she wasn't brought to your hospital."

While he sits on hold, waiting to be transferred, he will think over and over and over and over again: What good are we as humans if we give up on the lost? How can we live with ourselves?

BOOK FOUR

LUCY

THE MORNING OF the thirty-first day that she wakes up in a hotel on Highway 15 in Victorville is the day she decides to go home. Over the last month she's been wracked, afraid, angry, and lonely. She's been tired, wearied, beaten, and weak. And she's had her share of days believing herself the fool for squirreling away in hotel rooms as though somehow that will stop the world from turning—or, perhaps more pointedly: like being a deep-frozen cadaver waiting for future science to find a cure that will bring her back to life. But on this morning, Lucy opens the curtain to a blue sky that frames the desert so clearly, and so delicately, that she can imagine being able to poke a hole right through it.

For the past week, it has been building, a yearning to return. The realization that the essence of Henry is in the life they had together. Not where he last stood.

The longing has come particularly at night, when she's gone to bed, turned off the bedside lamp, and let the yellow glow from the lights along the highway sneak in under the curtain and wash over the room. There she'll lay awake in a dark that's not quite dark, hearing the cars and semis motor by, more and more aware that she's been living on a desert highway, a point between where people leave home to get somewhere else, or that they are passing through in order to get home. It makes her feel stupid and afraid to have found her life so removed and isolated. Each morning, after getting up, she'll look out on the parking lot, and she'll see all the cars. Behind them she'll see the stretch of highway that fades into the desert, and each morning she'll convince herself a little more that it is time to go home. She'll start to work through the particulars and unknowns, imagining not only the emotional mathematics of returning, but also the practical aspects of the legal case and of family and of work. Fixed in front of the window, she will run and rerun the details in her head, not noticing the maid knocking and her gut turning and the rain falling and the clouds clearing, not noticing that she's been caught in a perpetually circular question, asking herself over and over and over and over and over and over again: Can the disappeared ever really reappear?

But on the morning of the thirty-first day that she wakes up in a hotel on Highway 15 in Victorville, she is resolute. This is the day she decides to go home.

•

The afternoon she left Sacramento, walked out of her office, gathered her clothes and drove off, Lucy didn't have a plan. It was a culmination. A reaction. A moment. It was nearing the anniversary of the attack, when everyone around her seemed fixated on drawing her away from the immediacy of what had happened and into their own ideals of a resolution (the lawyers with her as the distraught wife, her friends trying to help her move on, the bass player and his judgment, the forensics man, Amy and her public performance, Henry's parents and the cemetery man and the desire for a ceremony). Lucy needed something else. Because after a year of managing the bureaucratic aftermath, and believing the people around her expected her to be strong, determined, and brave, the truth was that she missed him. She hadn't been ready to *accept*. She didn't want to live within the confines of memory, or have to be content with remnants and artifacts—the museum of Henry. Instead, she needed to live within what she'd imagined to be the living spirit of him. And so she drove south, heading in the direction where he'd last been, and she'd last seen him. She wasn't crazy; by now she knew that any physical traces were combed and sifted and catalogued—but those also only were artifacts, ones that could be airlifted or trucked away. That's not what Lucy was looking for. She was heading for somewhere impossible to know. The place where his essence still hovered. But who knew where it actually ended up? It may not be at the exact site of the attack, but she believed it was near there (certainly not near their home), and so she kept driving and driving and driving, as though being guided as some kind of dowser with her divining rod, waiting for it to bend and point.

•

Despite the yearning to go home, there is one major caveat: last night, on the evening of the thirtieth day that she woke up in a hotel on Highway 15 in Victorville, the television news reported that the trial of Ryan Mohammad Khan was getting ready to start; moving into the jury selection phase by the middle of the week. And just after that news broke, Attorney General Hopkins, now Republican Senate candidate Hopkins, held a campaign rally in an Orange County high school gym, the basket upturned above his head. Shifting his rhetoric to going to Washington to protect Californians against the threat of terrorism, he found the audience easily stoked by the deliberate and slow churning machinations of the Khan case. He walked a fine line between praising the hard, hard work of the good people in the U.S. Attorney's office, and condemning the bureaucrats and hacks above them for strangling justice in order to play politics. "While I'm glad to see some movement in the Khan terrorism trial," he said, "the lethargy of how it's been proceeding speaks volumes about the weakness of my opponent." His roar reached a fever pitch. "Despite failed US policies, over the past twelve years she has been nothing more than a rubber stamp for the president." Then the candidate paused. He lowered his voice into a low barrel-chested tone, leaned in, his lips nearly grazing the microphone. "This is about people, folks," he appealed. "People who are just going about their everyday lives, trying to get by, and then, I mean, wow, look what happens . . . Welcome to Radical Islam, ladies and gentlemen." As a reminder, he told the story about the young husband named Henry going to a conference a year ago, not more than a couple of hours north of here. His voice began to rise again. He said the young man was doing everything right, and then . . . Next, AG Hopkins invoked Lucy, saying that to her it was a "disservice and disgrace to treat that Islamic terrorist like a common criminal." He talked about when he'd sat with her. Seen the loss and confusion in her eyes. Said she couldn't understand why her government left her behind. Why it seemed like her own leaders were more focused on seeing Khan live than their own people. For Lucy's sake, justice should have been a swift action that sent a message about our strength. And as attorney general, he's battled for people, even if it meant fighting against an entrenched system. Slowing down to deliberately emphasize each word, he said this election was about fighting and standing up for people like Lucy. "Rubber stamps, folks. Nothing but rubber stamps. These are not just statistics, these are people." He said her name again. And the audience started to chant: *Lucy, Lucy, Lucy, Lucy, Lucy.*

Lucy had watched the whole rally broadcast live on cable. It was freaky. Surreal. Especially because it looked convincing. The mischaracterizations, the lies about the one time they met. The AG clearly believed his own fiction. Even Lucy found herself searching her memory for something she might have said to him, hunting for some telling expression she might have made that would've countered the reality that she wanted Ryan Mohammad Khan to live. Not out of pity or compassion. Not out of morals or ethics. And not for answers. She simply wanted Ryan Mohammad Khan to live because he was the only person who could keep the story of the day alive, and as long as that day lived, then Henry's essence lived.

Hearing her name being chanted had only reinforced that going home also meant having to find a way to distance herself from the U.S. Attorney's office, the attorney general's senate campaign, and every other industry dedicated to keeping that version of the past alive.

Only then could she begin to redefine herself.

She'd turned the TV off when they started chanting her name. Tried to forget about it. But throughout the day, and even when she lay in bed trying to go to sleep, she heard her name being intoned. *Lucy, Lucy, Lucy, Lucy, Lucy.*

•

The morning of the thirty-first day that she wakes up in a hotel on Highway 15 in Victorville she takes what's left of her clothes out of the drawers (she dropped off nearly all the boxes at a Goodwill box in a Safeway parking lot somewhere near Buttonwillow), and lays them on the bed, folding them into neat piles. She snatches up a sloppily folded t-shirt and refolds it several times, not quite getting the sleeves to square the right way.

In the mirror, Lucy catches her reflection. With her hair now dyed deep black, she barely recognizes herself; it makes her look so pale, as if her face is receding. Other than having liquidated half her savings into cash, changing her hair color was the one tangible step she took toward disappearing. She had done it several weeks ago when she'd first thought about venturing out beyond the hotel room and neighboring convenience stores. At a local CVS she'd bought the deepest black she could find, and then spent the next three hours prepping and rubbing it into her hair, the dye sometimes seeping through the plastic gloves and burning the bottom part of her palms that she hadn't coated with a streak of protective chapstick. By the end, after the dye had set, and after she'd rinsed and washed her hair, Lucy dried it, aiming the blow-dryer at the newly colored underside in order to give it more body, thinking that the hue turned out more blue than black, like the color of a comic book superhero's hair. She then auditioned names to match her new look—Sandy, Ella, Melissa, Jennifer—but quickly gave up, knowing they wouldn't fool anyone if even she couldn't get past her own ridiculousness.

Taking one small step forward, her knees brace against the mattress, cushioned by the rumpled bedspread. Lucy jiggles and shakes the t-shirt until it opens up again, and then she begins to refold it. This time holding it against her chest.

Swiftly, and almost out of nowhere, a solution to last night's caveat pops into her head. An impulsive call to action. Aloud, she declares, "If I'm going to go back, then I am doing it on my own terms." She looks for confirmation, as if the woman in the mirror might understand what she intends to do and then nod in approval.

Lucy drops the folded shirt back on the pile and grabs her throwaway cell phone off the nightstand, one she's only used to leave messages for her parents to tell them not to worry.

She turns on the TV, but mutes the volume. For what she's about to do, she doesn't want to be alone.

From memory she dials the phone number, starting with the 855 area code. It's a direct line, and when it's answered hello, she dispenses with any pleasantries, knowing the tenuousness of control. "It's me, Ray," she says.

The images on the TV change quickly during the commercials. A couple in a bathtub set out on a ridge. An old man chewing down on a corncob.

Ray just responds, "Lucy."

She waits a beat, but he isn't going to say anything more. She says, "I'm thinking of coming home."

He asks where she is.

"I've been a lot of places." She can picture him checking the caller ID, only to see that like her former doctor, she's learned how to make it read Private Caller.

He says, "We've been worried sick about you. Thrown us all. Hold on, let me see if I can get Margaret on the call."

"Please don't."

"She'll want to know. There is so much in motion right now."

"I'd really rather… Not right yet. Not today."

Even a mention of the trial would remind her of the adult child returning home and regressing into age-old battles. Your experiences and accomplishments have little value when cast back into a preset narrative. What she fears most of all is that if she engages any more, then she'll find herself willfully playing the same old scared widow role. In that light, this call was a risk. But like a vaccine, there are some cases where you need to submit to infection in order to ward off the disease.

Ray says, "Well, either way, it's a good thing you called." He can be heard rummaging through papers. Clicking on a ballpoint pen. "Did you tell me where you were?"

Why would she say that she is about eight miles from the U.S. Penitentiary where Ryan Mohammad Khan is being held, and only forty-or-so miles from where the attack took place? She's probably not even that far from him. "I just want you to know that going forward I'm not going to be part of the case."

Ray pauses. Breathes heavily like he's exerting himself. Is he writing notes to someone? "I'm afraid it's a little more complicated than that," he says. "It's not so easy."

She says she knows. "I've been following it on TV. Did you hear the speech last night? Did you hear them chanting my name? You can't be okay with that."

Ray says Hopkins's campaign is Hopkins's campaign. He makes his own rules. "But I can assure you that he is a strong ally with us. He told you that himself. When we met together. He wants justice for you as badly as we all do."

She can feel her heartbeat racing. Lucy tells herself to keep calm, not to come off like the crazy one. Pacing back and forth, she stops at the bed, scoops up the t-shirt with her free hand and then lets it flop back down on the pile of folded clothes. She needs to end this call. It seems impossible that she'll be able to maintain her composure for much longer. "I just need you to tell him that I don't want to be a part of it."

"You are misreading this, Lucy." Ray then reminds her the Ninth Circuit is under the Department of Justice, and has no direct line to the state Attorney General. "However, like the rest of this team, I assure you that Whit Hopkins is determined to battle terrorism. That's all. And as part of that battle, he understands the importance of the outcome of our trial. He's trying to help. Really."

"*Your* trial," she says, sensing all her discipline slip away. "Not *our* trial."

"Come on, Lucy."

"No. I quit . . . I quit. I quit. I quit."

"I know it's frustrating. A lot of pressure. But this is not a situation where you can just opt out."

"Are you even listening?"

"Lucy, this is more serious than you know. It's bigger than you know." The gentleness of his prior tone with her has given way to the stiff and firm shade of authority. The good cop act is over. But his voice also sounds suddenly distant and reedy.

She asks, "Am I on speakerphone, Ray? Have you put me on the speakerphone?"

"Listen, Lucy. You need to call me as soon as you get home. Do you understand? You will be compelled to testify, and it's just easier for all of us if we can get back to where we were. Let's remember why we're doing this in the first place. Why we've been in this together from the start. Just remember back to before this past several weeks. We're almost there."

"You didn't answer me, Ray. Am I on speaker-phone?" She can barely believe the forcefulness in her tone, as well as the ease in which it comes.

"You need to phone us as soon as you are home. No one wants to see this come to subpoenas and contempt of court, especially as, in the end, it only helps out Khan and the defense."

"To whomever is listening with you: I am calling you now. And, as I said, I only called to make clear that I do not want anything to do with this trial, anything to do with this senate campaign, anything to do with this anything."

In the background, papers shuffle. Computer keys click.

•

It isn't until she is packing the last of her box that she realizes they will be waiting for her at her house. She could kick herself for not thinking ahead. For losing her self-control. They'll never leave her alone. Not with the trial about to start. Not with the campaign happening, and the rallying behind her captivating the cable news cycles. Not when they know she is returning.

She considers calling Sarina. Maybe she could hide at her friend's house. Lay low for a while. These stories always have a limited shelf life. Let it blow over. But quickly she dismisses that idea. They'd certainly be on to that, if they're not already anticipating it.

While she just wants to get home, it's like all the roads are washed out, and the only way to clear the route is for her to get out and lie across the gap in the road, and let her own car drive over her.

Lucy lifts the box off the bed. In it, she puts her purse, the throwaway phone, and a message pad and two pens she's taken from the desk. It's everything she has.

The nagging thought comes back: Can the disappeared ever really reappear?

Once in her car, Lucy turns right, and drives north up Highway 15. At Air Base Road, a few miles up, where the prison is, where Khan is being held, she turns left. She slows down as she passes Victorville Penitentiary, a commanding complex on the desert floor, set against rocky hills and a low mountain range lining the horizon. She glances at the gates, almost as though she might see Ryan Mohammad Khan piddling around the grounds, alone and lost, and looking for company. If she were to see him, she swears she'd jump out and hop the fence and try to touch his hands. Hold them for only a moment, feeling the heat radiating through them into hers. Just after the entranceway, past the guard tower that is reminiscent of an airport control tower, she steps on the gas, gunning the engine.

Minutes later, after a half mile or less, she finds herself in the town of Adelanto. She needs a little more time. Not just out of fear of Ray and the U.S. Attorney's Office, but also because this is where it all is, everything connected to Henry's last days. Instinctively, she understands that never in a hundred-thousand-million years will she ever come back here again. This is her last, long goodbye.

Lucy pulls into a Days Inn. Carrying her box into reception, she says she'd like a room. The clerk asks her for how long. Lucy asks, "Can we take it day by day?"

THE FIRST TIME she sees it is in the Days Inn in Adelanto. From the edge of the bed, the morning after she checked in. Gripping the remote in her hand, Lucy keeps her thumb posted on the volume button.

All night long she'd been replaying the conversation with Ray. She'd been so resolute. Confident in what she saw was her right. But as she went over it in her head, she could only think of a game of checkers, one where your opponent lets you make your moves without opposition, seemingly unnoticed even, and then suddenly you look down at the board, and not only do you not have a move, but your entire strategy is being scotched. Where was that moment in her call with Ray? All night she asked herself that. When would he make his next move? Why hadn't she been more vigilant about not being played? How stupid had it been to think she could ever have had the upper hand with the federal prosecutors?

As she'd fallen asleep, she thought that maybe she should have listened to the bass player. His read on it had been right—they *were* all in it together: the U.S. Attorney, the Attorney General, the Republican National Committee. A true collusion. To them, everything in the world was a potential opportunity. A possible rung on which to plant their feet and pull themselves up higher and higher, and get more and more power to create their own agenda, not follow someone else's. And they could yack about justice, and they could flap their gums about bringing closure for Lucy and her family, but

215

in the end it merely was a story that had been cherry-picked and focus-grouped to create the most winning narrative. Think about it: they'd even been willing to withhold information about the bone chip because it confused their storyline, all the while in cahoots with a Senate candidate who whipped his base into a frenzied Lucy chant like it was some kind of righteous and noble anthem.

Nothing should surprise her.

But the first time she sees it she is as stunned as when the breath gets knocked out of you. There it is, her photo on the television screen. Blown up and close up. Followed by a snapshot of her and Henry, taken right after their wedding. A graphic in the corner that reads *Vanished Widow*.

Ray and his cohort have made their move.

She inches up the volume, hearing a newscaster on the local CBS affiliate explain that a disturbing report says there is concern that Lucy is missing. The newscaster is young. She is Latina, and her very demeanor and the assurance in her delivery predicts a fast trajectory to a major market and on to the network news. Her shoulders stay sharp and commanding as she looks into the camera, an authority that is enhanced by the way she narrows her eyebrows, draws down her lips, and gives a slight but judgmental shake of the head, suggesting the shame of tragedy. For more, she hands the story off to a reporter from their Sacramento affiliate who is standing outside the Archives. Speaking loud and rushed, the affiliate reporter explains that Lucy has not reported to work for several weeks now, and then it cuts to a prerecorded interview with Stache Man, sitting at his desk, a shelf of mismatched books and blue and red binders behind him, saying that given the anniversary of the attacks, they had assumed Lucy had been taking some needed time off, but when she failed to show up after an undisclosed amount of time and didn't return phone calls, he notified the authorities.

Ask him, why now? Lucy is thinking. *Ask him, why are you just saying this now?*

The interview cuts, and before the affiliate reporter throws it back to the desk, she reminds the audience that this all "comes on the brink of the trial of Ryan Mohammad Khan, the sole surviving suspect;" her sources tell her that Lucy had been slated to testify, but given this latest circumstance, will we be seeing a trial without its key emotional witness? Will the ongoing residuals of the attacks, such as the apparent breakdown and disappearance of the widow only reinforce the case against Khan, in this, a trial made more controversial by the introduction of the death penalty? Or will it hurt it? Either way, she concludes, she will be following this story as it develops. Back on camera, the anchor still is shaking her head. "A year later," she sermonizes, "and a sad reminder that we are still feeling the effects of that attack on our community in so many different ways." And then she turns to her colleague who has appeared beside her, a man in a slim blue suit with black hair so tight you can see the tracks from the comb's teeth, and she says, "But, Darren, it looks as though we have a beautiful week ahead."

Lucy flips briskly through other channels, and far up the dial, near the cable news stations, she catches a glimpse of her photo, just as they are cutting away.

She sits through the commercials, stupid ones for stupid drugs, and stupid local lawyers and stupid local car dealers and stupid local furniture dealers, and when the news show returns they go straight to a wildfire in the Colorado hills. However, along the crawler at the bottom of the screen she reads her name scrolling by, with a similar description of what she'd just seen on the local news, noting the clever turn of phrase: *The widow of the only missing victim is now also missing.*

She is squeezing the remote so hard she could break it. It's as though she has to tell her fingers to let go.

She holds back every instinct to call Ray. Tell him he's a son of a bitch for calling her out publically in order to salvage his trial, especially since he knew her intention was to come back, *not* to disappear. Tell him that he may think it's in the name of justice, but his outing of her only will ruin her life, forever casting her as unstable, when, in fact, she is as stable as she's ever felt since the attack, and that that stability is what gave her the strength to decide to come out of hiding, and to call him in the first place. But he wouldn't care. It's all business to him. For Ray and whoever else was involved in this, the rationale always is that justice is a system that is larger than individuals, and sometimes the meting out of justice means that there are casualties, but always in service to upholding the rule of law. Mostly she knows that calling him would only set her up for something else. She can't play with the likes of him. He is much too sophisticated. Cagey. And now with his leak to the media, for the world to see and judge, he's created a new reality, three possibilities, each of which can serve his case: either she remains disappeared, she agrees to testify, or she reappears as a fragile, permanently destroyed person.

Maybe, she thinks, that partially answers her lingering question about the reality of reappearance.

She kills the TV, watches the screen disappear into black, and then tosses the remote behind her; it lands on the pillow, right in the indentation from where she'd laid her head while she'd slept.

Other than last night's clothes and her few toiletries, her box is packed. She hadn't touched it since check-in. From the desk, she swipes another notepad and a pen, and the full box of Kleenex, laying them atop the box. Next, she goes into the bathroom to gather up her toothbrush, toothpaste, hairbrush, and her limited cosmetics. She also adds in the unused bottles of shampoo and conditioner and mouthwash. For good measure she takes an extra roll of toilet paper.

In the mirror, with her dyed black hair and consequently paled face, she sees herself as looking nothing like the kind and nearly innocent young woman in the photos she's seen broadcast. Only a slight resemblance, where, at best, she could maybe be taken for the bad sister. She probably looks different enough to avoid being spotted, at least in brief interactions. Still, she will take no chances. It's why she takes any extra provisions she can—from pens to toilet paper. There may be nights she's forced to sleep in her car. In an abandoned house or building. Anybody is recognizable to people looking to recognize them.

After picking up all the items to haul to her box, she makes a face in the mirror—an exaggerated expression of terror with big slapstick eyes and an elastic mouth stretched into a scream.

•

Backing up in quick but deliberate steps, her box against her chest, she sidles out the front door to the car parked right outside the room. The security lock has folded forward, blocking the door frame and keeping the door from closing all the way. She doesn't bother to fix it. She doesn't have time.

Three doors down, she sees a cleaning cart, but otherwise no one else is outside.

She shoves her only belongings into the back seat, and scuttles into the front. There will be no checkout. Nothing that will bring her into contact with anybody. She turns the ignition; the car starts into a low rumble, like an empty stomach in the morning.

The maid pops out of the doorway from three rooms down, takes a pair of towels off the cart, and then goes back in. The solitariness of her work only makes Lucy feel more lonely.

Starting to back up, Lucy shifts into park. She jumps out of her car, dashes to her room before the maid will reappear, and snatches one bath towel and one hand towel. At the last second, she grabs the Do Not Disturb sign off swinging on the door handle. Back in the car, she tosses the towels onto her box, and then rings the Do Not Disturb around the gear shift, laying it upward so she can see it at all times.

A month ago, she'd just needed to disappear for a while. Now, she considers, she actually is among the disappeared.

SHE IS JUST driving. Not even certain of what direction she is going. In the Mojave, the roads stretch on and on, and the landscape, both barren and hilly, kind of swirls like a wind with no particular direction around the valley desert floor. She breezes through towns that pop up, short passageways of fast food restaurants, gas stations, and soft serve ice cream stands. Some have local grocers; some have larger strip malls anchored by a chain market.

After two hours of straight driving, she stops to fill up her gas tank. The town is a replica of any one of the several smallish ones she's been passing through. At the entrance to the station are a row of arborvitae, the greens faded and almost translucent.

Pulling all the way forward to the last pump nearest the exit, she brakes, and then reaches under her seat for her cash. The money is hidden at the bottom of a plastic bag from a convenience store, the top layered with garbage, mostly used tissues and a couple of wadded candy wrappers. Blindly, Lucy picks out two bills, hoping one is a twenty. She doesn't want to count it in public, but she can feel the stash dwindling down. If this adventure prolongs, there still are the credit cards. And should those max out, there is some more savings, and the SSI she receives as a survivor's benefit. But those last options involve being visible and present. For the time being, this is what she has, and she'll have to be mindful and cautious about stretching it.

With a tank of gas, a bag of chips, two chocolate

bars, and a full water bottle, Lucy drives out of the gas station lot, turns right, and continues on in the same direction she'd been heading. She stutters through a series of stoplights trying to get out of town. Once outside the city limits, she stays in the right lane, cruising at a constant pace while other cars whip past her on the left.

The desert opens up again. She glances down at the gearshift. *Do Not Disturb.*

Fiddling with the radio station, she searches for something other than country music or the news. What she'd really like is a song from her high school days— maybe Vampire Weekend or Arcade Fire; she'd even settle for a pop-ish song that ran amuck through the school halls, like Lady Gaga's *Telephone*, or Coldplay singing *Viva la Vida*, or even Drake doing *Best I Ever Had*—something she can turn up, and sing along with so loud that it feels as though that is the force that actually turns the world.

But it's a bad spot for the airwaves.

•

Without realizing it, she's ended up on 89, heading north. The desert floor seems to be narrowing, or at least the mountains appear to be encroaching.

It's like gliding through a canyon.

Still unable to find a station she's willing to listen to, Lucy accedes to the silence.

Above, the sky is clear, with only the occasional contrail that wisps by, masquerading as clouds.

Driving and driving and driving, she tries to fight

off any feelings of shame that creep up on her. Driving and driving and driving, she tries to remind herself that she is the victim of the tragedy. She bears the brunt of the attorneys' reaction to her backing out. Remind herself that she is not the problem. And yet somehow, no matter what she tells herself, she feels as though she is. Lucy—the one who causes problems. Who can't deal with the world, and yet somehow is responsible for some part of its downfall.

·

The first sign to get her attention is for Yosemite. Her muddled route is now gelling in her memory. She remembers that eventually she will end up in the Sierra, and a turn leeward to the west on Highway 50 will dump her right back into Sacramento.

There are other options. Veer east across the Nevada state line and keep going all the way to the southeast to her parents' house in Durham. Or hang a U-turn and head south to Vegas.

But now, no more than six hours away, all she really wants is to be home.

Being pulled northward is not the struggle; that's what she wants. The question is what she'll do once she arrives. Will she battle and stand her ground about the trial, not wanting to see Ryan Mohammad Khan executed, in order to let Henry live? Or will she acquiesce, knowing it will free her from scrutiny and allow her to mourn in peace by allowing Henry to die?

At this rate, she only has a matter of hours to sort it out. And although she's tried to go at it alone, stay within herself and not drag anyone down with her, Lucy also realizes that she is outsized and outmatched.

On the shoulder of the highway, partially in her lane, a big vulture-like bird is picking remains off the asphalt. Just as her car rumbles so close she could hit it, a second and then a third bird swoop down beside the vulture, scaring it off just as the front bumper flashes by. Looking in the rearview, Lucy sees the vulture return to the otherwise clear highway, content with going back to its meal. It is that very moment when Lucy knows what she has to do.

Near the town of Bishop, she pulls over into a fast food parking lot and takes her phone out of the glovebox. A carload of teenagers sits across from her: two boys in the front seats, and two girls in shorts, untucked flannel shirts (one red tartan, the other blue), and flip-flops standing outside the car on each side, leaned forward and chewing, elbows braced on the window frames. For a moment, Lucy is overcome with jealousy, witnessing them laughing and posturing, with no concern for anyone else, completely unfazed by the hundreds of miles of empty desert that surrounds them. She tries to tamp down an emotional combustion of anger and sadness, wanting something more for the girls, who look smarter than the boys, yet willfully default to bashful idiocy because it must seem better than being alone.

Lucy punches in the Sacramento area code, and then the next seven numbers. If she's remembered her schedule correctly, Sarina should be on break, away from the research desk or even her own office. As she taps the final number with her index finger, Lucy sucks in a deep breath, and closes her eyes. She keeps them shut while the line rings. She doesn't open them until she hears Sarina pick up.

"Oh my god," Sarina says. "This is the weirdest thing." And again Sarina repeats that it is the weirdest thing. She says, "Swear to god I was just thinking about you. I mean *just.*"

Lucy says she needs to be quick; she's in a parking lot in the middle of nowhere.

"Are you safe? Are you okay?"

One of the boys has tossed a wadded up bag toward the garbage can, missing it. The girl on his side glances at it, starts to move toward the trash, but then turns back and again leans into the window.

Sarina says she's walking. She says, "I'm heading downstairs and out of the building so that we have some privacy. If you hear noises, it's because I'm walking. That's what you're hearing. Maybe it will make it safer. Too many ears perking up around this place."

"I really need to be quick, Sarina."

"I've seen those reports on the news, and I know they are bullshit. Complete and total bullshit. I'm livid *and* apoplectic over the lies Stache Man is telling. Total, total, total BS."

The wadded bag blows against the base of the garbage can. The girl in the red flannel is watching it, as is Lucy while on the phone. Each gust of wind makes the trash bump against the bottom of the can, as though it could plow its way through.

"Sarina," Lucy says, "I need to ask a favor of you."

Through the phone line comes the rumble of the light rail. The ringing bells. The hissing of the door

225

opening. The flood of people pushing in and out; their silence, when heard en masse, is loud and vociferous. For a moment, Lucy is there—reaching her free hand out, as though she will touch it.

Sarina keeps saying her name over and over. She's almost shouting, the reception has become as muddled as talking between two tin cans connected by a string. Just as quickly, it clears up. Sarina says they broke up for a minute. Maybe a dead zone. "Can you hear me now?"

Lucy drops her hand, and grips the steering wheel. She repeats herself. She says, "I need to ask a favor of you."

The girl in the red flannel looks back to the garbage can several times. Finally, she pulls back from the car window, says something to the boy, turns around and walks over to the trash receptacle. She kneels down without bending at the waist, her long and thin legs collapsing like hinged girders from an erector set, picks up the boy's garbage, and drops it into the can.

IT's a PLAN, but not much of one. Still, Lucy has to credit her: Sarina was swift and decisive. It makes Lucy wish she'd been a better friend to Sarina all along. Before the attacks, she'd tolerated her in a friendly but distant way, as one often does with people randomly brought together through their jobs. Then after the attacks, she had leaned on her to some degree, too involved in her own struggles to even consider giving anything back. In fact, Lucy can't think of one time that she asked how Sarina was doing, or what was going on in her life. Now, without thought or hesitation, Sarina is there for her again. Willing to take chances. And, given this new legal tactic of public exposure, willing to put herself on the line.

The plan Sarina developed was this: Sarina would book a hotel room for Lucy, so Lucy could land in town without the pressure or risk of exposure. It would give her space to figure out the next step. Even if there wasn't an immediate solution to anything, at least Lucy wouldn't have to be alone with it.

It wasn't so much that Lucy believed the feds were staking out every hotel or intersection. But with her name and face having been splashed across the TV, she didn't need some overly ambitious desk clerk trying to make a few bucks on the side, either by tipping off the local news or by shooting ready phone footage.

Neither could remember the name of the motel, but they both understood it to be the one with the big, giant red sign off Highway 80 in West Sac. A trucker's hotel. Off the beaten path. Sarina would be waiting in the room. Upon arrival, Lucy would phone from the lot. Three rings and then hang up. Then, Sarina would flash the lights twice. It worked in the movies, she said. Why not it real life? For an extra precaution, Sarina said she would make the reservation under her mother's name, using her mother's credit card as a deposit. On the way over, she'd pick up food.

She didn't want Lucy to have to worry about anything more than getting there.

•

Back on 89, the rumble of the road gets to her. With few options, she finds an AM news station that is hosting a call-in show. It's the best she can do. The topics range from the California drought to the recent unemployment figures to whether the farm subsidies are enabling a broken system that's only setting up the small farms for an eventual collapse. And then the conversation turns to the pending trial of Ryan Mohammad Khan. Lucy's instinct is to turn it off. Tune it out. She knows she's become a character in someone else's costume drama. But she keeps listening. Not out of some form of torture or anything, but more because she's curious to hear what people think of her. What they are willing to say.

Her thoughts wander back to her mother and father, no doubt hearing many of these same things. She knows she's neglected them; it's been enough just to contain the constant pressure from Henry's parents. They must be worried sick. Last year, when her parents had fielded calls day in and day out from regional reporters looking for a local connection to the West Coast attacks, psychically, it nearly had wrecked them. More than once, they had told her how relieved they were when the hounding ended. Now, Lucy can imagine how easily it might start all over again. Not just the regional media, but the national media ringing the phone, knocking on their door, camped out in front of her parents' driveway. She needs to leave a message for them right away, and then call as soon as she settles back into Sacramento. Imagine what is being asked of them in this latest round: going from the tragic loss of their son-in-law, to *their* missing daughter.

The host, smooth-voiced and deceptively upbeat, reminds the listener that the topic of the trial has come up because of this morning's comment from one of the defense lawyers. In an interview in *The Los Angeles Times*, the lawyer complained that this recent blast about the missing widow made his client less likely to get a fair trial. Already, the lawyer reportedly said, public sentiment is stacked against his client, without a thread of evidence having yet been evaluated, and that reports such as this have so little relevance. And then, according to the radio host's summary, the defense attorney stopped just short of outright accusing the U.S. Attorney's Office of planting the story when he referred to the missing widow story as the product of a "systemized bureaucratic lynch mob."

Most of the callers' sentiment focuses on Khan deserving to die and candidate Hopkins's speech (with, of course, an audio clip of the Lucy chant), which quickly devolves into a few exchanges about the larger issue of the death penalty, weighing its moral obligations against its potential efficacy in dissuading future criminals. It swings back and forth between the actual and the conceptual. But it's what is not said that most catches Lucy's attention. On occasion, someone will mention "the widow," but, despite the sideshow of her photo and her alleged disappearance, the fact is that, at least based on this call-in show, she is inconsequential to people's concerns about the case. She has been someone else's tactic. Apparently a failed one, at that. And while she is fully aware that the prosecutors still are willing to ruin her, either to compel the testimony or dismiss its lack thereof, at least she knows that in the minds of listeners to a call-in show in the Central Valley of California, the first strike has been a total failure, and, with that failure has risen the increased possibility that she will not be quite as invisible, not quite so disappeared.

•

The ride into Lake Tahoe and down through the Sierra toward Sacramento was familiar and comforting. She and Henry had made the drive on many occasions, preferring weekends in Tahoe to the almost equidistant trip in the opposite direction to San Francisco. They liked the ski resorts in the summer, taking the lifts and gondolas to the peaks of the mountains and hiking the trails down to the base, with daypacks filled with sandwiches and candy. Dinner often was on a deck overlooking the lake, the two of them like a pair of small planets in an inverted galaxy.

Coming down 50, Lucy caught the last light of

day, with sharp rays cutting through the tops of the pines, as though the beams were angling for her. And along a stretch of road past Echo Summit, the charred trees from a recent forest fire looked nearly enameled, patterned in deeply cracked coal with webs on the surface that appeared as though they could've been hand drawn. She'd been forced to close her windows. Despite the fires having been contained and ended several weeks ago, the residue of the smoldering, sharp with the odor of destructive decay, smelled as though it only had been snuffed out last night.

Near a wide switchback at Pyramid Creek, Lucy pulled over and left a voicemail for her parents, assuring them she was okay and in control. Staying in her car, she watched the sunset over the mountains. It looked less like the sun going down and the day fading away, and more as if the night were pushing it down.

IN THE MOONLESS valley ahead, the lights from the buildings cast a glow over the Sacramento metropolitan region, hazy and dome-like.

In less than twenty minutes she will be at the motel with the big sign on the highway.

In less than twenty minutes, she will pass by the exit that leads to her house.

In less than twenty minutes, she will reappear.

•

Here's the funny thing: she'd been two miles past her old exit before she noticed. And it hadn't made her feel bad or negligent. It didn't make her feel as though she'd let down Henry or his memory. Instead, she'd laughed. Actually burst right out loud in the car, something she really couldn't remember doing in ages, not even with Henry. It was a characteristic she'd always envied in others, taking it as a sign of genuine warmth and connection; in contrast, her laugh always came out sounding conscious and rehearsed. But driving up 80, after hours of stewing in pent-up anticipation and expectation, she turned nearly hysterical for a moment, like an audience member watching her own show, perched on the seat, roaring and clapping when the punchline finally comes.

•

Creeping along the frontage road, she looks for the driveway into the motel. She doesn't know West Sacramento at all; her only lasting impression of it was as an industrial warehouse area just over the river from downtown. Tonight, several semis are parked on the street. A fast food joint lights up the corner, and a little farther down a bright yellow sign from another hotel cuts through the haze. It looks like any other urban block in the early evening of a moonless night.

Finding the entrance, Lucy pulls in to the lot and stops in the middle. It's nearly empty, only a handful of cars and pickups. The motel and its grounds look so small and compact compared to the huge sign that looms over it and faces the freeway.

A single row of rooms bends in an L-shape. To the right, opposite the arm of the L, where the building ends almost at street-side, is a fenced-in swimming pool with only three white strapped chairs. It's hard to imagine who would swim there.

A few of the rooms are lit by an orange-ish glow against the drawn curtains. But most are dark.

Lucy punches in Sarina's phone number, and she lets it ring the planned three times. And then she waits.

And she waits.

The whole area is completely dead. Where is Sarina's flashing light signal? It's starting to feel a little fishy. What if Sarina didn't come? If something scared her away?

The rumbling of the idling car reminds Lucy she could peel off at any second.

A man in jeans and a white t-shirt appears out of a nook near the office. He's slightly hunched, which looks more wearied than physical. Crossing in front of her headlight beams, he glances once at Lucy, both hands trying to steady an overfilled ice bucket. A few cubes fall out and land in front of him, causing him to step gingerly around them.

The Iceman cometh, she whispers to herself.

He then disappears to the left, at the end of the L, and into his room where the light flicks on. *And now the Iceman goeth.*

This is getting ridiculous. Lucy phones once more.

At the farthest end, almost opposite from where the Iceman entered, and in front of the swimming pool, finally the lights flash twice. It's a slow pattern, with a long enough pause between flickers that it just as easily could be someone fumbling at wall switches, trying to find the right one.

Lucy double clicks the high beams.

The Iceman parts the curtains, peers out to check on the disturbance, and then pulls them shut. Seconds later the lights flash from the swimming pool room, following the previous pattern.

•

Sarina pulls her inside, closes the door and then hugs her. "It was hard to see," she says. "Through the fence, the swimming pool fence. Plus, the trucks parked on the street. It was hard to see . . . And, oh my goodness, your hair."

Lucy tells her it's fine. She's here. As for the hair, she says she knows. Believe me. But it will grow back. It always does. They are standing between the end of the bed and the door. Hotel rooms have become familiar to her. So much so that for being back home, she could be anywhere.

For the moment, they are silent. Waiting for the other to speak. It is as though all the effort and worry and energy has been directed at getting Lucy here, and now that she is here there is no sense of what they are supposed to do. Much less what comes next.

Finally, Sarina pats the edge of the bed. "Sit down," she says. "Sit."

Lucy nods, obliging her. For the moment, glad to be led.

Sarina steps around her, and walks between the dresser and the bed, stopping short of the bathroom. She kneels down, lifts up two grocery bags, and swings them onto the mattress, near the pillows. "Other than cheese," she explains, "I didn't get too many perishables. I didn't know what the situation would be." She takes a baguette out of one bag, pulls the paper sleeve off it, and then tears it into four pieces, laying them atop a napkin she unfolded, pulling it right beside Lucy. "Please," she tells Lucy. "Go ahead."

Lucy breaks off the end of one of the quarters, and slowly chews it.

At the sound of a neighboring door slamming, Sarina glances to the window. She holds her position. A few minutes later, she whips her neck around when she sees headlights cross the parking lot. "I guess I'm on hyper guard alert," she apologizes. "You never know."

"You never know," Lucy says, leaning forward, elbows on her knees. And then she thanks Sarina for everything she's done.

But it doesn't appear Sarina is listening. After hearing a car door shut, followed by the chit-chat of two men and their jangling keys, her attention is drawn back to the window. She inches over and peers between the curtains, barely opening them at the center with her right index finger. Her left thumb and forefinger rub back and forth at her hip. Like a mute cricket. "It's nothing," she says. "Don't worry. It's nothing at all."

Here's what is, Lucy thinks: It's a lousy situation. One they'd misread. They thought they'd been sneaky, when in fact they are like two runaway children, seeing if they can hide out until sunrise before their parents catch them. Lucy straightens up, and declares this is stupid. A really dumb idea. And it is really unnecessary. Again, she thanks Sarina. But she says she just should go to her home now. This is stupid, sitting completely paranoid and on edge in a West Sacramento motel only minutes from her own house.

Sarina steps away from the window. If Lucy didn't know better, she'd swear Sarina was blocking the door. "That," Sarina says, "would be nuts. In a million years, I'd never let you do that. Not tonight, at least."

Lucy fixes herself tighter to the edge of the bed, hands braced against the mattress. Her heels lift a bit, propping her on the balls of her feet. "Why not tonight?" she demands to know.

"You don't think you can just show up and have everything return to normal, do you?"

"But why tonight? I don't understand what it is about tonight."

Sarina won't seem to budge. Her only movements are a slight turn of the head in response to another

236

outside noise. "Tonight," she says, "is because there is no plan beyond tonight. *This* is the plan."

Lucy lets herself go, falling backwards on the mattress, landing on top of the pieces of bread, her head propped between the two shopping bags. It's as though she's still in motion, the engine still vibrating and buzzing through her butt and lower back. She rolls slightly to the left, reaches under her, and pulls away the napkin with the bread pieces to the side, and then lays flat again. She thinks of Maine lobster traps, the ones in which the lobsters crawl right through a welcoming entrance, and once they reach the bait in back, they realize that the return passageway is too narrow at its entrance to get out. But unlike some other kinds of animal traps, the lobster trap is not meant to do the exterminating. It only is meant to catch and hold. What happens next is in the hands of the captors.

Yes, she supposes, Sarina is right. *This* is the plan.

WHEN HER EYES open the next morning, a little groggy, a little confused, her first sensation is hearing Sarina say, "Oh good. You're up."

Sarina is sitting in the reading chair by the window. The room still is dark, but Sarina's face is shaded blue from her phone's screen. Her eyes glow, lit up, wide awake and waiting. The sound of the freeway roars in the background.

"Did you sleep there all night?" Lucy asks, covering her mouth as she yawns.

Sarina jumps up, and cracks open the curtains in the middle, enough to let in some light. Lucy shades her eyes. She's like those cave dwellers who could go blind at the first exposure to sunlight. Sarina walks in front of the bed, stopping at the TV on top of the dresser. In the dim light, she pats around the base, knocking a pamphlet to the floor, and then comes up with the remote. She says she's been waiting an hour for Lucy to get up. "This news is incredible. Completely and totally unexpected."

Lucy flattens her palms on the mattress and pushes herself up against the headboard. She inhales through a short yawn, still waking up. "Please tell me you didn't sleep in that chair all night."

The television pops on, and Sarina hushes her, holding the remote against her lips. "Listen," she whispers. "Let's listen."

It is the same cable network where, after first watching the photos of herself on the local broadcast,

Lucy had landed and seen the "widow" crawler. At first, nothing is registering. There is a host sitting with three guests at a round table, and a fourth guest in Washington, residing in a bubble at the top of the screen. It all sounds like chatter.

Lucy is trying to make out why this is of importance. What she's supposed to be listening for. Just as she's about to ask, a photo of Ryan Mohammad Khan flashes across the screen. It's one of the same three that always gets shown—a picture probably lifted from Facebook, a selfie where his face looks disproportionally wide, eyes narrowed, and his lips defiantly pressed together, with his head cocked. In another context it might be seen as comical, a parody of tough street culture by a man-boy whose simple haplessness is apparent at once, neither tough nor sophisticated, only a costumed appropriation of a culture that never would have him. But in the current context, he is the star of this role. The epitome of evil. The face of depraved detachment.

Sarina asks, "Can you believe it?"

"I really don't . . ."

"Well, just pay attention."

Lucy tugs up the comforter, just below her chin. She makes herself listen, even though she really doesn't want to hear.

It appears that the prosecutors are dropping the death penalty against Khan. In the bottom corner of the screen, a video clip starts up of U.S. Attorney Margaret Kelley speaking at an earlier press conference. Ray is positioned behind her. Arms folded over his chest, he looks disgusted, as though being forced to apologize for something he doesn't believe he did. As Ms. Kelley reads a prepared statement, Ray manages to hold his head high, while he keeps his gaze willfully downward. The TV show has cut the volume on Ms. Kelley, reducing her to a mumble in the background. The panelists talk over her. Already by this hour they've seen this clip a half-dozen times.

From what Lucy can get, a deal was struck overnight, and while the specific terms of the sentence have not been disclosed, just prior to the press conference it was officially released that the death penalty no longer was on the table.

She focuses on the TV; she really wants to see the shame in Ray's eyes before they cut the video.

The second most used Khan photo comes on, the one from Iraq, where he is in full-on khaki gear, gazing at the camera with a Kevlar helmet and wraparound sunglasses, posed in front of a tank, one hand on the barrel of his M16, the other on the trigger. Fuzzy in the background is a bombed-out building.

Lucy reaches behind her and folds her pillow in half, wedging it under her neck. No matter how much she adjusts it, she can't seem to find the proper support.

The inside word is that this unprecedented deal came down to the phones. Much of the prosecution's case had been based on portraying Khan as an active member of the assault, the architect who phoned in movements and directions to the actual assailants as he watched it unfold on the television from his couch. His phone records had shown several calls dialed out. That was not in dispute. But what did appear to come to light followed the unlocking of the two shooters' smart phones, something that had taken FBI hackers the better part of the last eight months to crack. And, according to leaks from within the Bureau and from within Justice, based on the length of the calls, most lasting less than one second, it showed clear indications that no conversations reasonably could have taken place between Khan and the assailants. There was no question that he knew the shooters, and likely had some prior knowledge of the terrorist attack. But the idea that he had been a mastermind had been debunked, reverting back to everyone's first instinct that Ryan Mohammad Khan had been nothing but a simpleton caught up in something he probably didn't understand as anything more than a video game come to life. Still, it was understood that he'd be going to federal prison as an accomplice. He just wouldn't have a trial. And he wouldn't be executed there.

Number three photo pops up with a large white type caption that reads *Plea Deal Reached in Khan Trial. Federal Prosecutors Say No Death Penalty.* The host, more concerned with the larger implications, shifts to how this development might reflect on the president, the attorney general, and the political futures of all those others who had staked out a position on this case, using the word *overzealous* to describe their rush to judgment in order to show a decisive response to the attack and to would-be terrorists at home and abroad.

Whit Hopkins is interviewed. A real coup for him to be the top-of-the-hour interview on a national morning show. He says this turn of events is disgusting, and it proves the whole system is rigged in favor of the Radical Islamic Extremists. The underlying shame, he adds, is that the U.S. Attorney's office is filled with good people who are hampered by the political correctness of the executive branch. This is what happens when the congressional agenda is to rubber stamp, rubber stamp, rubber stamp.

Lucy says to turn it off. The sheet nearly covers her mouth. She can taste the bleach.

"Don't you want to hear more? It's remarkable."

"Please. Please just turn it off."

Sarina slowly lowers the volume until the TV mutes. But she leaves the show on, her eyes jumping between the bedded Lucy and the updating crawler. It's almost touching how giddy Sarina is to have Lucy back. When the news program goes to commercial, Sarina declares, "Coffee!" She mimes an old man hunched over at a diner, sipping his mug, and then buzzing up once the caffeine hits, arms winged out with vibrating fingers.

It makes Lucy smile, even when nothing is quite making sense. She says, "I forgot how stupid we can be."

Sarina's arms now are in front of her, stretched out as she lumbers toward the coffeemaker, muttering in her best Frankenstein voice, "Coffee . . . Coffee . . . Coffee."

As good as it is to keep Khan alive, and as good as it sounds to get the specter of the testimony off her back, Lucy asks herself, what really has changed? What will she do?

From the bathroom, Sarina fills up the little carafe in the sink. "Coffee . . . Coffee . . . Coffee."

A loud, thrusting blast of water.

It will be hard enough just to get out from under the covers.

COMING OFF THE freeway on the 16th Street exit, Lucy rolls down the windows. Ever since she left the motel, she's felt like she stinks of cigarette smoke. She lifts up her arm, sniffing the sleeve of her blouse but doesn't smell anything other than vague traces of the many leftover odors of a series of hotel rooms. It's as if the pungency is coming from inside her face.

At the stoplight, Lucy checks in the rearview to make sure Sarina has kept right behind her. When they left the motel, Sarina offered either to keep on going if everything looked okay at the house, or she could come inside with her once they got there. Really, whatever Lucy wanted. Lucy said she thought she could handle it alone. But she'd see once they arrived.

Sarina wiggles her fingers in a wave.

Maybe the smoke smell is something imprinted on her brain. She's heard about people who've suffered a trauma being afflicted by weird sensory malfunctions. At least the outside air is refreshing. A cool morning, clear with clouds drifting in, and a breeze that shivers the leaves. People are out walking. Biking. The fresh air doesn't quite kill the odor, but it does neutralize it a little, making her hope the cigarette smoke smell is just something on her clothes or in the box of stuff in the back seat, not from something in her head.

Nearing Broadway, a car slips between her and Sarina. As cavalier as Lucy had been about going at this alone, her shoulders tighten and her breathing shortens. She keeps looking behind, trying to see around the 4x4 that has cut in. She can't imagine losing Sarina right now. Not in this unpredictable world. Lucy rolls the window up, walling off the outside.

Suddenly everyone out walking and biking on the streets looks foolish and naïve. All the threats of the past year mean nothing to them. Step by step, yard by yard, alone and negotiating their separate spaces as though each controls that piece of their world, Lucy marks them all as vulnerable. They are like victims of a plague who don't know they've been infected, and won't know it until it is far too late.

Behind her, it's impossible to see anything but the 4x4, deep black, and driven by a woman in a peach workout shirt, one hand on the wheel, the other pressing a phone against her ear, talking nonstop.

Sarina fights for position, veers into the other lane, cuts her nose across the center dividing line, and, with her blinker on, she pushes her way in front of the interloper, claiming her rightful spot.

Lucy watches her wave again. This time with a smile and a wink. It's hard to tell if it's for Lucy or for the driver of the 4x4.

Sarina tightens up, so focused on staying close that she probably doesn't notice that Lucy has turned left on Broadway. That she's heading all the way down to Freeport so that she doesn't have to go near the cemetery. And she probably doesn't notice that once on Freeport, Lucy will swing right on Castro into the neighborhoods, and then a quick left on 2nd Avenue to Harkness and up to Caramay, essentially driving circles around every block, each one marked by bungalows with matching lawns and towering Valley Oaks and English Elms, all in order to prolong her arrival.

Sarina won't know how hard it is to shed a reeking odor when you think it could be coming from inside you.

•

Parking in the driveway seemed too familiar. Too forward. And so she pulled up curbside, stopping right in front of the walkway.

Across the street, Holberg's sprinkler is drenching his lawn. It weaves back and forth across his front yard, falling in all directions due to a constant breeze. His rich green grass stands in sharp contrast to the yellow and brittle blades that make up her yard—the welcome mat of the abandoned.

She's here.

She's home.

And it's all right. It's okay.

Sarina edges in right behind her, bumpers almost touching. She knows not to park in front of the neighbor's house. People are funny that way.

•

Release the seatbelt.

Remember to close the windows in case it rains.

Turn the car off, and don't forget to take the keys with you. Put them in your purse.

Lift the lock, and open the door.

•

Standing on the sidewalk, Lucy looks across the street. There are lawn signs for Hopkins on both sides of Lucy's house, no doubt a well-intentioned neighborly nod of solidarity. She swears Holberg and Lady Holberg are monitoring her from behind their living room plate glass window.

She turns her back on them, making sure to stand straight and confident so that they can't say anything different when they retell the story.

From inside her car, Sarina gives the thumbs up. Lucy pauses and looks at her. She's not sure this is something she wants to do, go into this house. But then again, she considers, it might be even weirder if she actually wanted to.

Perhaps picking up on the ambivalence, Sarina splays all her fingers, tilting her hand side-to-side *más o menos*, her face puckering into a question mark. Lucy nods, mouthing *it's okay*. She then turns and goes up the walkway, between the yellow and brittle lawn with the towering Valley Oak whose branches dip and point at her with just a hint of judgment.

Being at the front door feels so strange and so unlikely.

For a moment she just stands there, taking in deep breaths, reminding herself that this is her home. Repeating it like a mantra. This is her home. This is her home. This is her home. This is her home.

It's why she is here.

Holberg and Lady Holberg surely are watching, dying to know what she's going to do, betting that she doesn't have the will to go through with it. Still facing the front door, Lucy takes her keys out of her pocket, and holds them up over her shoulder in a clear display of intent.

But she still can't seem to move.

Sarina calls something out through the open window, startling Lucy from her spell. Leaned across the passenger's seat, Sarina says it again, her face wrenched in an expression of concern. It is something along the lines of *not mind* and *no shame*, but Lucy can't hear, lucky enough to make out even those few words against the brushing leaves and the nonstop winds.

"I can't," Lucy calls back. "I can't hear you."

Sarina says it again, but her words still come out muddled.

"Can you just come up here?" Lucy waves her forward. "Just come here."

Sarina slips out of the car, heading up the walk. Fallen leaves cascade past her feet, whipping in circles, while never leaving the lawn.

A cloud pauses in front of the sun, muting the daylight. At almost the same time the wind dies down. It is a giant pause. Like being in the space between two frames. And then, as though unleashing a cumulative hoarding, a giant gust bursts forward, rattling the branches of the old oak and drawing out a low moan from its brittle trunk.

Lucy's keys jangle. And her hair whips up at all angles, blowing a long dark strand over her eyes. For a split second she can't see Sarina. She can't see Holberg and Lady Holberg. The street. The Valley Oak. The *Hopkins for Senate* signs. Or anything.

SARINA'S SNEAKERS SQUEAK against the living room floor.

Is she pacing?

Once they'd gone inside the house together, Sarina had decided her job was to be the lookout. Meanwhile, Lucy would face returning to her bedroom for the first time since leaving. "Call the cops if I'm not out in fifteen minutes," she said over her shoulder while inching down the hallway, trying to modulate the shaking in her voice.

From the front room, Sarina's main task is to keep watch for media. Nosy neighbors. Lookie-lous. That was the plan. Ten minutes ago. Since then, nothing has happened, and Sarina only sounds restive. At the threshold of the bedroom, Lucy sucks in a deep breath, ready to step inside. She just needs to get it over with, and not allow the history of the room to overpower her ability to move on. But she is distracted by Sarina's pacing, thinking her friend is expecting her to fall apart. Finally, she hears Sarina flop onto the couch. Then, on cue, Lucy steps forward.

There is the TV where she saw the very first images of the shooting, and then later the bombing. (The screen still is lit blue; when she'd bolted out that afternoon, she must have turned off the cable box without turning off the television itself.) She doesn't see the bed, instead she sees a corner of a bed, the place she sat while watching that coverage. And she sees a bedspread that couldn't quite cover her enough. The edge of her nightstand is not about the last book she was reading, or about the yellow lamp, or about the photo of her with raised hands on the edge of a hill in Wilmington overlooking the Atlantic—it is about where Sarina's first call came in, alerting her to the news. She sees the edge of the top drawer of the dresser that got slammed in frustration. The route that she wandered between the window to the closet door to the bed and back while on the phone with Henry's parents for the millionth time about needing to secure a burial site and plan a ceremony.

Lucy's breathing is getting short, wheezing from her chest. In a way, being in the bedroom is a lot like entering a stuffy museum. Or maybe like moving through a series of memories that both are dormant and alive at the same time. The room is too stagnant. Too still. She starts for the window, to let in some natural light and reawaken the room. But then she hesitates. Sometimes the most innocent step into a wilderness can end up disrupting its entire ecosystem.

This is stupid, she thinks. She's tempted to call the Goodwill. Easily, she can picture herself standing on the front steps and waving them forward, flatbed backed into the driveway, a low branch scraping the hood of the cab, directing the men back to the bedroom, watching them haul the items down the hallway and making sure they don't bang the walls on the way out. She tells herself all the stuff in the room are objects, just a collection of random pieces that barely add up to a single memory, no more full of life than any others on a thrift store shelf. Lucy pulls her phone from her pant pocket; she's pretty sure she will actually call. She's pretty sure she can live with tossing out the last witness to Henry's life at home.

Down the hall, the couch springs squeak. Sarina must be shifting. Getting up. Restless despite her endless patience. Sarina calls out, "Five minutes until I call the cops." Only then does it even occur to Lucy that Sarina had to have taken the day off from work for her. And for what? So Lucy can walk back in to her house? And now Lucy's left her out there alone when she just wants to help. A wave of lousiness washes over her. As much as Lucy needs a friend, she needs to be a friend. "Hold on, I'm coming," Lucy calls out, slipping the phone back into her front pocket. And then she says it again, this time singing it with the melody from the old Sam & Dave song. Sarina yells back that she's such a goof. Why are we always such a pair of goofs?

Before going back out, Lucy inches around in a complete circle, a final lighthouse beam taking it all in. It's as though she needs to catalog every aspect of the room before she works up the nerve to call the Goodwill. Freeze it in time. Label everything. Name it. Find context and continuity. But after turning a third of the way around, the prospect proves itself impossible. There is no single moment. No unique event. Every inch of space, every artifact, is more than the star of its own scene, it is its *own* solar system all together. And none of it is ordered or linear. Much like memories, everything she's seeing crisscrosses and weaves in and out of the other, driven by its own muddied narratives.

But there is one thing that is clear. Perfectly clear. She sees no trace of Henry. On that morning just about a year ago, it's as though every trace of life in the house was wiped clean and tossed away.

And that, she thinks with more than a tinge of guilt, actually is quite, quite liberating.

THE MORNING OF the service is the first day she'll go out in a while. Already Lucy had been growing increasingly nervous about being out in public again. Following wall-to-wall coverage of the terrorist attack in Nice carried out by a single driver and a barreling cargo truck, her daily routine had been thus: get in the car, drive to work, eat lunch inside the building with Sarina, get in the car and come back home. She kept out of public spaces. Avoided any kind of events or gatherings. She'd made one trip to the farmer's market with Sarina, on a Saturday morning, on a blocked off section of 20th Street, and just entering into the condensed crowd, the rows of tables, the barriers at the end, and the children dashing in and out while dogs lowered and growled at one another, nearly had sent her into a tailspin. It forced her to sit on the steps in front of a skate shop, trying to gather herself and catch her breath, and then, unable to find Sarina who had wandered off in search of strawberries, Lucy eyeballed every opening for the quickest escape route out. She might actually have come undone if Sarina hadn't spotted her, and, immediately noticing the panic in Lucy's eyes, whisked her out of the crowd without a question being asked. Later, when all was calm in Lucy's living room, Sarina was kind enough not to say a word about it—not then or ever again.

But on the morning of the service, Lucy is alone, and when she's alone she moves a little more languidly. Takes her time, even when she knows she shouldn't. It's a little cloudy out, making the morning a bit darker than normal. It is fifteen minutes before the hour, and she needs to allow ten minutes for the drive to the cemetery. The extra five minutes seems like all the time in the world. Her parents are taking a taxi straight from the airport, and Henry's parents, who arrived late last night, declined to be picked up, saying Lucy shouldn't have to run a shuttle service on the morning when they'll be burying the memory of her husband. They would rent a car, which it seems they did, as she hasn't heard a word from them other than a brief text from the airport (that she didn't see until this morning) that read, *Arrived!!!*

Although she is at the point where she should be starting the car, Lucy still is in her bathrobe, clothes laid out on the bed. Her hair is combed; her eyeliner on. Like a superhero, she will only need to slip into her costume. She keeps glancing at the phone, expecting it to ring. Someone wanting to know if she is okay, because they thought she'd be at the gravesite by now. But she has time. She has five minutes before she is running late. And stupid as it is, she's a little disappointed that no one is checking.

On the morning of the service, the television still is the antagonist; she's kept it off for days. It is the object that enables her to never set foot out in the world again. And she doesn't want to be like that. She can't be like that. In fact, things felt pretty manageable until she heard about this Nice attack, and she'd made the mistake of gluing herself to the screen all night long as pundits guessed at answers and motives, running the same hectic cell phone images over and over, zeroing in on the father and son who died together until that snapshot of the two of them was drilled into her brain. Until then, she'd been able to be back at work at the Archives, a return to her job that in part had been negotiated by the lawyer friend of Sarina's, who, among other things, had unconventionally but successfully argued that Lucy's month of abandoning her job was a collateral consequence of the larger issue of the trial, the loss of her husband, and the trauma of the terror attacks. And perhaps, even more than what went on in paper negotiations, was the clear understanding of the Secretary of State's Office that not letting Lucy return to her job would appear as heartless and unpatriotic as defecting to a hostile government. This especially was heightened when information on the possibility of Lucy losing her job was leaked to *The Bee*, and the story ran on the front page—both in print and online.

She rises to her feet, not allowing herself to fall into the sinkhole where she feels herself descending. She slips out of her robe; it melts onto the floor into a red terrycloth puddle. There she stands in her slip and bra, looking down at the dress she will wear, black, appropriately black, bought only days ago, as she lost almost all her nice clothes when she'd dumped them in a charity box somewhere on the Grapevine. Suddenly a superhero costume doesn't seem like such a stupid analogy; indeed, she thinks, that is exactly what that dress is—something that will imbue her with the power that allows her the strength to go out into the world, and to get through the pain of the ceremony, which may not be painful just for revisiting the loss, but for what the occasion will take with it, namely Henry.

But then again, and she wouldn't say it to a soul, not

even Sarina: maybe the ceremony can be something of a celebration of a reappearance of Lucy, as well.

If only.

The nightstand clock shows her with two minutes to go until she needs to be leaving. Lucy stands hands on hips, still in her undergarments. The leather straps of her shoes curl and snake from under the bed. Outside her window, cars rumble down the street. She hears a red wagon grinding over a sidewalk, bumpy from rising roots, and a child's voice narrating and laughing. She hears doors slamming. Lawn mowers churning. Dog collars jangling. But what she doesn't hear is security or safety. It is not comforting at all. She only hears risk. And vulnerability.

At work the other day, Sarina had asked if they should walk down to Capitol Park and eat lunch outside. The day was beautiful. Being inside seemed like a waste.

Lucy said she didn't know about doing that.

Sarina, figuring Lucy might be worried about being recognized, said, "It's okay, no one will notice."

What Lucy didn't say, what she wanted to say, was that was exactly the problem. No one will notice. That is why strangers walk into a building and shoot and bomb other strangers. Why a man driven by ideology can plow his truck through a boardwalk full of people. Because no one will notice that they are people. And how easily they can disappear. They merely are objects. Pins in an ideological blowing alley. And in fact, she wanted to add, she'd likely be more inclined to want to be out if someone *will notice*, because then she might feel like she'd have a fighting chance. But instead of saying something, Lucy had looked away from Sarina. She said her stomach was a little gurgley, which wasn't altogether a lie, because since she started thinking about it, her gut had become more than a little upset.

She looks down to the phone again; its screen remains blank. And yet somehow she knows that she needs to put on the dress, gather up the strength and go. If she can get through this ceremony, then she knows she will come out okay on the other end, with her fear buried along with Henry's memory. Maybe then she will be able to, finally, reappear.

She will do everything she can do to avoid going to the cemetery. It is not because she wants to hold on to everything, it simply is because she can't imagine being there. After the announcement of the Ryan Mohammad Khan plea deal, the forensic archeologist had been back in touch with her. He'd made no reference to his standoffish demeanor the last time they'd spoken; the reasons were understood. But he'd told her he had the results, and he prefaced it by saying he was sorry, and then informed her that the lab tests, straight from the 6750 Freezer Mill, had come back inconclusive; and she asked, Does that mean that it is not Henry? and he began explaining the process of how they do the matching, and how many matches it takes to make an identification with an authentic profile, and that due to the degradation of the bone fragment (remember *black-burnt* v. *blue-gray burnt*) that it was, as he said, inconclusive. And she asked if it *seemed* close enough to claim it as Henry, enough so to inter it and bury it at the cemetery. He said he couldn't answer that, it was a question that left the measures of scientific inquiry, partially lodging itself between morality, ethics, and epistemology; what he could comment on was the practical side: first, she needed to remember that it was only traces of dust now (*the extracting and grinding*), and also he didn't even know if the governing body would release any of it to her, especially with no sound basis for the claim on her behalf, given that its results were inconclusive. He said he could check, if she'd like. She said she'd think about it. And she never phoned back. The whole thing felt too funny, if not a little bit unseemly.

Without something to bury, the service was becoming more and more of a memorial for Henry's parents. She never would have denied them that conclusion. Then her parents elected to fly out because they too felt they should be there in support. Sarina, a few other relatives from both sides of the family, and friends of Henry's next joined the small but growing guest list. Soon, all the talk became of closure. It was the word the minister from the Unitarian Church used in the planning. It was the word both sets of parents used. Sarina said it too. Closure. And when somehow the funeral plans leaked out to the press, it too became the word that everyone in the public sphere defaulted to. Friends, family, and strangers. Closure became the word for everyone to take solace in. Except for Lucy. Because for her, closure meant being closed into that past, along with Henry.

And that was terrifying.

Since she's come back from her escape, all she's wanted is to reappear in a world where people see her as normal, and she can see them the same, without being steeped in fear and trepidation. But she fears that the service will only memorialize the disappeared Lucy, a so-called closure that is nothing more than a permanent seal. Frankly, no one is capable of seeing her otherwise. And, even more worrisome, is that she's starting to believe she'll never be able to see herself otherwise, either.

The clock has moved inside the ten-minute mark. Her dress, the black dress, remains laid out on the bed. If she were to slip into it right now, dash out the door, and into her car, Lucy still would be late in arriving. Maybe only a matter of minutes at this point, but nevertheless late.

But instead of dressing and leaving, on this morning of the service, she lowers herself back on to the bed, her eyes transfixed on the blank telephone screen. She glances at the clock and sees it is one minute before the ceremony is scheduled to start.

For just a moment, she is tempted to call Sarina, let her know she is running late, and that she will be there very, very soon. Sarina will take charge. Sarina will tell her not to worry. Not to rush. And she imagines Sarina will cup her free hand over the receiver, mouth to the group *it's Lucy*, and indicate that everything is okay, *Lucy's just behind schedule*. Her parents, Henry's parents, and the others gathered will nod, fully understanding. They may even be relieved. But what's worse to consider is that they will be expecting it. Not expecting it because Lucy always is late. Or that she is unreliable. She is not. They will be expecting it because in their world she has disappeared into the tragedy. They will think it is brave of her to even be there at all. They will take all the loose borders that she is trying tighten and stretch and stretch and stretch them, giving her all the space and depth in which to further disappear.

The clock passes just over the top of the hour. Finally, the phone rings, lighting up and buzzing like an alarm with a caller ID reading *Unknown Number*.

She sits up straight, answering it. First comes a cough, followed by the unmistakable voice of Edith Franks, first clearing her throat, and then speaking. It is a simple missive she intends to say; a conjoined tone of threat and disappointment. Edith Franks simply says, "I see you still have no respect or concern for the *time* in *scheduled time*." An engine noise takes over, followed by a blaring horn, and a fumbling yet abrupt hanging up.

Lucy rises, drops the phone, and leans over the bed. Lifting up her dress at the indentation along the waist, she slips it over her head, threading her arms through the sleeves. Once it's on, hanging a little looser off her hips than she'd remembered, she tugs and shimmies at the waist, adjusting it to just the right fit. She pokes a foot under the bed, and drags out each shoe.

Lucy starts to leave the house, but turns around to go back to the bedroom, having forgotten her phone.

The day of the service, Lucy will remember that Edith Franks has been the only person who's treated her as someone undefined by a tragedy. The only person who hasn't expected her to be guided and grounded by consequences.

And as she passes out of the bedroom, phone in hand, Lucy says aloud, "Edith, I love you too." As she did when she'd first thought that nearly a year ago, she isn't being ironic. Nor is she being sarcastic.

She only is reappearing.

About the author

Adam Braver is the author of five novels (*Mr. Lincoln's Wars*, *Divine Sarah*, *Crows Over The Wheatfield*, *November 22, 1963*, and *Misfit*). His books have been selected for the Barnes and Noble Discover New Writers program, Borders' Original Voices series, the IndieNext list, and twice for the Book Sense list, as well as having been translated into French, Italian, Japanese, Turkish, and Russian. Braver's fiction and essays have appeared in journals such as *Daedalus*, *Ontario Review*, *Cimarron Review*, *Water-Stone Review*, *Harvard Review*, *Tin House*, *The Normal School*, *West Branch*, *The Pinch*, and *Post Road*. With a joint appointment, he is on faculty and is Library Program Director at Roger Williams University in Bristol, RI. He also teaches at the New York State Summer Writers Institute.